ALSO BY LISA RENEE JONES

Infinite
Possibilities

LISA RENEE JONES

G
Gallery Books
New York   London   Toronto   Sydney   New Delhi

G

Gallery Books
An Imprint of Simon & Schuster, Inc.
1230 Avenue of the Americas
New York, NY 10020

First Gallery Books trade paperback edition July 2015

GALLERY BOOKS and colophon are registered trademarks
of Simon & Schuster, Inc.

For information about special discounts for bulk purchases, please
contact Simon & Schuster Special Sales at 1-866-506-1949
or business@simonandschuster.com.

The Simon & Schuster Speakers Bureau can bring authors to your
live event. For more information or to book an event contact
the Simon & Schuster Speakers Bureau at 1-866-248-3049
or visit our website at www.simonspeakers.com.

Designed by Davina Mock-Maniscalco

Manufactured in the United States of America

10 9 8 7 6 5 4 3 2 1

Library of Congress Cataloging-in-Publication Data
Jones, Lisa Renee.
Infinite possibilities / Lisa Renee Jones.—First Gallery Books trade
paperback edition.
    pages cm (The secret life of Amy Bensen ; 2)
    I. Title.
PS3610.O627154   2015
813'.6—dc23
                                                        2014045402

ISBN 978-1-4767-9384-9
ISBN 978-1-4767-9378-8 (ebook)

ONE

RAW AND HONEST.

That's what Liam Stone claimed he wanted from me—but it's not what he gave me. He lied to me. He hurt me. And still some crazy, stupid part of me clings to the idea that there could be a logical explanation for what I overheard between him and Derek last night. The same part of me that saw him as my hero, willing to fight my proverbial Godzilla.

But he was never truly my hero. And after a sleepless night in the Inn at Cherry Creek, I've faced reality. I can't risk trusting him—or anyone else—until I confront the past someone wants me to forget. That means leaving Colorado and my identity as Amy Bensen and heading to Texas, which is exactly what I'm working on now.

Entering a downtown Denver pawnshop on a gust of wind, I swipe my long blond hair from my face and glance around. The T-shaped glass display shelves are unattended, yet the all-too-familiar sense of being watched makes me want to turn and leave. This is where the guy at the flea market who made a cheap fake ID for me told me I can obtain a high-quality one that will allow me to disappear. And that's exactly what I need, because Liam Stone's money and power will enable him to hunt me down if I don't fully cover my tracks.

"Hello?" I call out, hugging myself against the air-conditioning. I'm chilly in the white shorts and red tank top I bought at Walmart after my dinner-turned-disaster with Liam last night. I hate that I can't go back to my apartment for my things—though most of them were bought by Liam, anyway. Once I'm able to disappear, I'll pull my money from my old New York account and purchase more basics that really feel like mine.

I move farther inside the store, praying the twenty bucks I gave the cabdriver is enough to ensure he waits for me. "Hello?" I call again, but my answer is more silence.

Seconds continue to tick by and I feel increasingly uneasy. Deciding to check on my cab and regroup, I turn toward the exit.

"Señorita."

I turn to find a burly fiftysomething man with a thick beard as gray and wiry as his longish hair. "I was looking for Roberto," I say. Is this scruffy-looking stranger my ticket to freedom?

He's in front of me now, the scent of cigarettes wafting off of him, his jeans and T-shirt wrinkled and worn. "I am Roberto," he declares. He reaches out and lifts a strand of my long blond hair, and it's all I can do not to shrink away from him as he adds, "My man said you were brunette."

I step back, tugging my cheap, oversized purse in front of me and between us. "Wig," I say. "I brought it with me."

"For a quick change of identity," he comments. "Smart, mami."

I don't know what *mami* means, but after the horrid ID his man at the flea market made me, I decided I needed a better disguise. In a worst-case scenario, I can still pass with my Amy Bensen photos.

"Twenty-five hundred dollars," he says.

I gape. "What? No. I was quoted five hundred."

"You need to disappear badly enough to want two hair

colors. That means you need the best identification I can make you. That runs twenty-five hundred dollars."

"I don't have twenty-five hundred dollars. What do I get for five hundred?"

"Nothing. You were quoted wrong."

My gut knots. "I don't have that much."

"Well, then," he says, his lips thinning, "use your flea-market ID." He turns away, dismissing me.

"No," I say quickly. The fake ID his guy made this morning won't get me through a grocery line, let alone airport security. "Wait." He faces me again, arching a dark brow in a silent question. "I have seven hundred dollars."

"Twenty-five hundred."

My mind races, calculating how much I'll have left to survive with if I go higher. I settle on a firm "Fifteen hundred dollars. That's all I have."

His gaze rakes up and down my body, then returns to my face, and I feel violated. "Perhaps we can barter," he suggests. "You give me something I want. I give you something you want."

My heart lodges in my throat. I want to survive. I want answers. I want to make Amy Bensen disappear, but not like this. "No, I—"

"Yes," he counters, and his hands come down on my shoulders.

Panic rushes over me and a surge of adrenaline spikes through my blood. I shove his hands away. "No!"

He grabs my wrists. "It'll be good for you, I promise."

"Let go!" I hiss. A familiar prickling in my scalp begins, signaling one of the dreaded flashbacks that can debilitate me. "No. *No.*" Pain spikes along my scalp like a blade. "Oh, God. Not now."

"Oh, God is right," he promises. "Over and over, you gonna say that."

I see the intent in his eyes. He isn't going to make me an ID. He's going to make me a victim, if I let him. I'm sick and tired of being everyone's victim.

I raise my knee hard, putting every bit of my strength behind the blow to his groin. He grunts and doubles over, panting in pain. The prickling in my head is more pronounced and I shove against the door, desperate to escape before I collapse. A quick glance to my right tells me the cabdriver has deserted me. I run blindly, as fast as I can.

Spots splatter in front of my eyes, and I dart into a diner and head for the sign that reads "Restroom." Once I'm inside the one-stall room, I lock myself in and press my back against the door. Pain pierces my scalp and I ball my fists and slide down the door, just in time. Suddenly, I'm flashing back to the past.

I park my Toyota Camry in front of the house, thinking

about what it'll be like to be in college a few months from now, with no curfew. Stepping outside into the hot Texas night, I realize that the porch is dark. How very . . . odd.

I frown and shove the car door closed. My parents' Ford SUV is in the driveway. Since my mom isn't on the porch waiting to tell me I'm ten minutes late, maybe the migraine she was fighting earlier caught up with her. Still, I feel uneasy, and pull my keys out to be ready.

Quickly walking toward the house, hoping to avoid a lecture, I tiptoe up the porch stairs. The third plank creaks loudly and I freeze. Dang it, this is Dana's fault. I told her I had to leave the movie theater thirty minutes ago, but the captain of the football team was talking to her and she's infatuated with him.

I rush up the rest of the stairs, and the instant I hit the porch, a hand wraps around my upper arm. I gasp and a big hand covers my mouth. I reach for it, trying to pry it off of me. A second later I'm pushed against the wall, the hand still over my mouth. "Were you inviting someone to grab you and hurt you?"

I blink my older brother into view through the inky black night, and his hand falls from my mouth. I grimace and lift my knee to his groin, stopping just shy of contact. "I should hurt you. You scared the crap out of me, Chad! When did you and Dad get back into town?"

He ignores the question. "When you see something unusual like the porch light being out, don't just charge forward and hope for the best. Walking around in your fairy-tale world of Saturday night dates and teenage gossip isn't going to keep you safe."

My anger is instant. "'Teenage gossip'? Did you really just say that to me? I want to be at the digs with you and Dad. I want to be exploring the world. It's your influence on Dad that keeps me from traveling with you—so don't even go there, Chad."

A lock of curly blond hair falls over his brow as he shakes his head. "Because I'm fucking trying to make sure you have the normal life I have never had."

I suck in a breath at the raspy, affected quality to his words that sends goose bumps down my spine, and fear clenches my gut. "What's wrong, Chad?"

He just stares at me and I wish like heck the shadows would soften on his face.

"Chad?" I prod.

He shoves off the wall and scrubs his face. "Nothing's wrong." He motions to the door. "Let's go in."

"Not until you tell me what's going on. And don't tell me it's nothing. Tell me the truth."

"You can't handle the truth. If tonight told me anything, it's that."

"That's unfair. I'm living the only life you let me have. What aren't you telling me?"

Pounding jolts me back to the present and I am on the ground, my legs spread out on the filthy floor of the restaurant bathroom. "Chad," I whisper, aching at how real he'd felt. Only months after that night, I lost him and everyone I loved. I squeeze my eyes shut, remembering how Mom had opened the door and ended the conversation that Chad never reopened. Chad had blamed his behavior on a girl and a bottle of tequila I know he'd never touched. I'd have smelled it on him.

You can't handle the truth. I'm ashamed of how right he was. Ashamed at how I've hidden from and blocked out everything for the last six years, afraid of what I'd discover. My lashes lift. Not anymore.

I open the bathroom door and return to the dining area, and it's as if the memory of Chad has shifted something inside me. I am suddenly challenged to be more than I have been, but deep down, I know this has been coming. Something inside me burns to escape the prison that's been my life. It is almost as if, on a subconscious level, I went to work at the museum to tempt fate and force myself to finally act.

Exiting the diner, I'm remarkably coolheaded about how to deal with my travel limitations. I hail a cab and direct the driver to take me to a bank. There I withdraw the cash from my New York account, knowing I'm sending out an alert about my location to whoever was following me from New York.

Next, I have the driver take me to Walmart, where I suck it up and invest in more of what I need for my travel plans: a selection of casual clothes, two small black suitcases, a couple of hats, sunglasses, and basic toiletries. After I pay for the items I go to the bathroom and change into jeans and a navy tee, putting my purchases in one suitcase and leaving the second one empty. Finally, I slip on a red hoodie to make sure I stand out at my next stop.

When the cab pulls up to the curb at the airport, my nerves are tight as I force myself to get out of the car. I have a plan, and it's a good one. Good thing, too, since there is no plan "B" that makes sense to me.

I head to the counter of a budget airline and snag a seat on a flight leaving in less than an hour. I check in the empty bag to make my reservation look more legitimate, keeping the other bag with me. Once I have my boarding pass, despite my feet resisting, I press forward, reminding myself that there are cameras and security personnel everywhere. I'm safer here than anywhere else.

Fifteen torturous minutes later I head to the gate, where

I claim a seat near the counter so I can call for help if needed. I do not move. I just . . . wait. And wait. And wait. Finally, boarding time arrives. This is where I have to do things just right. I wait in line, and the attendant scans my ticket and waves me down the ramp. I walk through the entryway and disappear onto the boarding ramp, then move to the wall, letting others pass. My hoodie comes off and I stuff it in my bag, then tug out the black ball cap I purchased and shove my hair underneath.

An attendant appears from around the bend in the ramp. "Do you need help?" she asks.

"My mother is meeting me, and I'm worried. Do I have time to look for her?"

"You have about three minutes. Is she a confirmed passenger?"

"Yes."

"What's her name? I'll call her on the intercom and check the manifest for her name."

"Kylie Richardson, and thank you."

She looks concerned and nods. "Give me a moment as we continue boarding. What's your name?"

"Lara," I say, speaking my real name for the first time in six years, and all but choking on it as I do. I don't let myself dwell on the foolishness of using it in an airport where I'm surely being hunted.

"Lara Richardson?"

Brooks. But for reasons beyond my obvious need for discretion, my birth name no longer feels like me. "Yes."

"Okay, Ms. Richardson. Go find your seat and I'll find your mom."

I follow as she goes up the boarding ramp and peek around the corner to see her walking toward the counter, where another attendant stands. The waiting area is empty. Like it had been the day I met Liam, when I'd thought I was going to be bumped, but instead ended up seated in first class next to him. Now I wonder if that was a coincidence, or by his design.

With the attendants facing away from me, I hear the announcement calling my fictional mother and I seize the opportunity and quickly leave the gate area. Then I all but run down the escalator and straight toward the taxi stand. There I hand the dispatcher a twenty-dollar bill. "I'm late to a wedding rehearsal dinner. I need out of here fast."

He glances at the money and nods. "You got it, sweetheart." He lifts his hand to motion to a cab and then grabs my bag.

"In the backseat, please," I instruct, wanting it where I can get to it if I need to make a fast departure. I can't afford to throw out any more money after the cost of that plane ticket.

I'm just about to get into the backseat when I hear someone say, "Amy."

For the flash of a moment, I freeze at the sound of Liam's deep, all-too-familiar voice. No. No. *No*. He cannot be here. He *can't*.

But he is, which can only mean one thing. He's been having me followed—confirming that he was never just a stranger who touched me deeply. He's everything I don't want him to be; everything I had prayed he wasn't.

I whirl around. Wearing faded jeans and an Izod shirt as perfectly aqua blue as his eyes, Liam looks every bit Mr. Tall, Dark, and Handsome. And he's close. Too close.

He moves forward and I hiss, "Don't!" and hold up a hand. "I'll scream bloody murder."

He stills, and our eyes lock, his narrowing, holding mine captive. "Run *to* me, Amy—not from me."

The words stir a passionate memory of him saying them to me once before. And they hurt. I hurt. "I don't even know who you are."

"You know who I am. Who are you?"

"Hey, lady," the driver says. "You coming?"

"Yes," I call out. "Yes. I am." But I don't look away from Liam. "I heard you talking to Derek last night."

"You don't know what you heard."

No denial. I wanted denial. Not hearing it tells me more than words, and I turn away and start to get into the car.

"Don't do this," he commands, but there's a hint of a

plea I'm not sure is real. Maybe I just want it to exist. Maybe I just want to turn back time and make last night, and so many things, go away. "You need my protection," he adds.

I laugh, but it's all pain and no humor. "Your protection was never what I needed." It was his honesty, his realness—which I now doubt.

"You need my protection," he repeats. "That's what I was talking to Derek about. Protecting you."

Is the camera feed live? he'd asked Derek. That isn't protection. "Lies don't protect me," I bite out.

"I didn't lie to you."

I grind my teeth at the realization that I want him to give me a good reason for what I'd overhead. *There is no good reason*, I remind myself, as I had a million times last night. I let my guard down with him, and I can't risk that. Not when my family's dead, and I could be next.

"I can't do this with you," I whisper, not even sure if he can hear me as I lower myself into the cab.

"I will find you," he calls after me, and the words are pure conviction, a promise.

"You can try." My heart is racing as I yank the door shut, lock it, and tell the driver, "Go—now!"

The car jerks into motion and Liam pounds on the roof. "Damn it, open up, Amy!" The private, always-in-control man I know is nowhere to be found. He runs alongside us, leaning into my view. "Don't do this, Amy. Stop, now!"

"Do we have a problem, lady?" the driver asks.

"Drive and we won't!"

He guns the engine to pull ahead of Liam, and his absence is both a relief and a blow. I twist around to stare at him, the baseball cap falling from my hair, my eyes desperately seeking Liam. He's running after us. *Running.* Liam doesn't seem like a man to run after anyone, but he's running after me.

My fingers curl into my palms and I force myself to turn around. Liam was desperate for me. It was in his eyes, his actions. His voice. And I'm desperate for him, for the man I believed had ended my eternal hell of being alone.

But I don't know *why* he is desperate for me, any more than I know why I am hunted, or how he might be involved. I only know that he could be.

And right now, I realize why I let six years pass before I looked for answers. Not knowing who to trust, or how to find out what I need to know without dying, is terrifying.

But not knowing was just a facade of safety—and it's simply no longer an option.

I will find you. Liam's words play in my mind. He will, if I give him the chance. My nails dig into my palms. If I ever see Liam again, it has to be my choice.

I sit up straight as we exit onto the highway, and I think of the note in the suitcase at JFK airport.

Be smart. Don't link yourself to your past. Stay away from museums this time.

BE SMART.

Calm slides through me, as it had after the diner this morning, and I'm back in the zone I found years ago to escape the memories of the fire that destroyed my world. *Stop and think, Amy. Stop and think before you act.*

I resist the urge to direct the driver to the first exit; it will be too obvious. "Exit here," I order several miles later, digging cash out of my bag.

The cab takes the frontage road. "Right or left?" he asks.

My gaze lands on a truck stop, and a lightbulb goes on in my head. "Just go straight," I order, tucking my hair securely under my ball cap. When he stops at the red light ahead of us, I open my door, tossing him the cash.

My zone does not seem to stop my adrenaline from spiking through my veins at the danger of being out in the open, a danger I'm ready to have behind me. Shoving my purse onto my shoulder, I dart across the road, my suitcase in tow. This new plan is much better than the one I started with this morning.

The instant I'm inside the truck stop, I make a beeline to the back door that I can tell leads to the industrial gas pumps for the big rigs. I'm bypassing my Plan A, which had been to buy a cheap car off of Craigslist, one I wouldn't need an ID to buy, and drive out of the state. Dangerous as it might be, I'm hanging onto my cash and hitchhiking, because staying in Denver any longer than necessary is dangerous, too.

I step outside to look for the most un-serial-killer–like person possible. As I exit, a short, bearded man in jeans and a cowboy shirt grabs the door and stops a few steps from me. "You need help, sweetheart?"

Already this is seeming like a bad idea. "No, I'm good."

He squints, revealing thick lines around eyes that spend way too much time moving up and down my body. "You need a ride?"

"She's with me."

I glance up to find a thin, fiftysomething red-haired woman kicking up dust with her cowboy boots. She stops beside me. "You ready to head out?"

The look she gives me is all motherly authority, and my heart is squeezed by memories of my own mother. "Yes," I say, no hesitation in my reply. "I'm ready."

She motions me toward a big red rig and I fall into step with her. "I'm Shell, honey. I'd ask what you're running from, but I'll spare you the lie. I ride with my hubby, Roy. You can join us if you like. Where you headed?"

"Away from here," I say. "That's all that counts right now."

Sadness seeps into her eyes and is quickly extinguished, but I see it. I feel it. Oh, how I feel it, and once again I feel a connection with a stranger. But then, all I have in my life are strangers. Who else would I connect with?

"Who do we have here?" a happy-looking gray-haired man with a beer belly asks as we approach the shiny red truck.

"This is . . ." Shell begins and glances at me questioningly.

"Amy," I say, clinging to the name that's the only thing I've managed to keep for six years.

"I'm Roy, Amy. You know how many truckers it takes to pump gas into a rig?"

"Ah, no. How many?"

"None. We make our wives do it."

Laughter bubbles from my throat, and Shell snorts. "He doesn't make me do anything, honey."

Ten minutes later I'm at the window seat of the rig with Shell between me and Roy, and my spirits have taken a nosedive. As Roy pulls onto the frontage road, a crushing sensation fills my chest, pressing against it like the big rig I'm riding in is rolling over me instead of the hot pavement. I feel no regret over leaving Denver, but there's plenty over leaving Liam. I still want my Godzilla-slayer—which is exactly why I need to put distance between us.

I don't know who I'm running from, or if I'm wanted dead or alive. I simply know I have enemies, and that it's time I find out why. And I'll do that by being my own Godzilla-slayer, the hero that honors my family the way they deserve to be honored.

TWO

Silver City, New Mexico
Population 10,000

"WHERE THE HELL IS AMY?"

I rush through the back door of The Dive's kitchen just in time to hear the question from our bald, often-cranky cook. "I'm here," I reply quickly, hanging my black backpack on the coatrack on the wall just inside the kitchen. "Ready for my shift."

"You're late," George grumbles.

Grabbing the hair clip on the outside of my bag, I wrap my hair into a knot at the back of my head and glance at the clock that tells me I'm actually two minutes early despite a flashback that had brought me to my knees. But I don't argue, just as I haven't done anything else to bring attention to myself in the past eight weeks. "Sorry," I offer, and Katy, the bottle-blond waitress who's been here three years to my two weeks, casts me a friendly, sympathetic look.

I force a small smile before cutting my gaze away and grabbing an apron to tie around the pink uniform dress that all the waitresses here pair with white tennis shoes. It's not that I don't appreciate Katy's concern. I like her quite a lot, considering I've been here such a short time, but I have no idea if we have anything but this place in common. Nor will I ever find out.

I'm here another week, tops; then I'll find a trucker who feels safe and I'm out of here. It's my only option until I have enough money and a well-researched plan that enables me to return to Texas without ending up dead like my family.

George flips a burger on the massive grill in the middle of the kitchen. "If you two are ready to work, go give the dinner crowd some holiday fucking cheer. We have turkey and dressing on the menu until Thanksgiving."

"It's Halloween," I say before I can stop myself, not ready for the holiday. Not this year. Not for the past six years.

"Close enough to a holiday for turkey," George grumbles. "I got it at a bargain, so go push it to customers. Now get to work. This ain't Halloween party time for you."

"Who needs costumes and parties?" Katy quips. "We have a monster in the kitchen every night."

George glowers. "I'll show you a monster if I have turkey left over."

Katy comes toward me. "The drunks in the dining room are nicer than him," she grumbles as we exit the kitchen behind the long counter where customers can sit instead of at one of the red booths or simple tables.

"I hope you're right on that one," I say, stopping as the scents of french fries and bacon mix like sour eggs. Suddenly my stomach clenches, then rolls.

"But you'll get used to him, I promise." Katy glances at me and her brows dip. "You okay?"

"I took a vitamin on an empty stomach—I should know better." As much as I hate all the lies that are my life, this one comes easily. The two waitresses ending their shift head toward us, and I barely register the exchanges that follow.

My mind is in another place, back in Liam's hotel room, where we had angry, passionate, unprotected sex. *I can't be pregnant.* Eight weeks, three cities, one period, and one negative test say I'm not. But my period was barely spotty.

When I finally head toward my first table, any comfort I've talked myself into ends when another whiff of bacon hits me and my stomach knots again. *Not pregnant*, I repeat. *It's impossible. Right?*

Just like working in a roadside diner on the run isn't possible, and yet it's happening. That's enough to make me decide I'll take another test during my dinner break. Until then, I hope for a busy crowd to keep my mind off of the moment when I look for that little pink line.

ALMOST FOUR HOURS later, I head toward the pass-through window behind the counter to pick up my last order before my break. Thankfully, whatever had affected my stomach is long past, but I still want to put my mind at ease. Most likely it's due to lack of sleep, worry, and the incessant flashbacks I can't control without the acupuncture I can't afford. But I'll fix that. I'm working on a plan that lets me get settled in Texas, pull myself together, and be on top of my game when I address the past.

"I think every drunk in town has come here tonight," Katy complains, joining me to wait for her next ticket to come up. "I've been groped and hit on all night, and that was just the women."

"Right there with you on that one," I say, and for some

reason I feel the need to promise myself this job, this life isn't forever. It's just a means to an end. It's smart. It's me staying off the radar and building resources.

Katy pats her apron pocket. "At least the tips have been good."

I nod in agreement. "I'm close to my best night ever. And I can use every dime I earn."

"Can't we all." Her gaze flickers over my shoulder and her lips quirk. "And honey, I have a feeling your tips are about to get better. As I was headed over here, a guy who looks real expensive and good enough to eat asked to be seated in your section. No offense, but I tried to get him for me." She glances down at her ample cleavage. "The girls failed me. I guess he likes them au naturel."

I go still at her words, and a familiar, too often repeated memory of me telling Liam I want to lick his tattoo flashes through my mind. He is not here. It can't be him. It just . . . can't. But isn't that what I said when he'd shown up at the airport? *Can't* isn't a word Liam likes. Can't never applies to him.

"Order up," George shouts and shoves two plates into the pass-through.

Staring at the plates, I will myself not to overreact. Not to create a Godzilla that doesn't exist when I have plenty of problems before me that do. Liam is not here. I've moved around frequently and paid cash for everything. I've found small diners to work in that will accept my pitiful "little girl with a lost wallet" excuse during the paperwork process. I promise to replace my ID right away and then write down a random Social Security number. Even the phone calls I've made to Texas to research my past were placed on disposable phones that I ordered with Texas numbers and a prepaid gift card. I've been smart. I am not traceable.

"You daydreaming, or doing your job?" George demands, snapping me back to the moment.

Grabbing my order, I whirl around, but my chance to scan the diner for the man Katy mentioned is lost when several people walk in, blocking my view of the rest of the room.

As I set the order on my customer's table, the sensation of being watched comes over me. No—the sensation of being watched by *him* comes over me.

Liam. Liam is here. No. No. No. He's not here. No Godzilla, Amy. No Godzilla.

"Can I get ketchup?" my customer asks.

I manage a choppy nod and turn away, taking a few steps before I stop dead, my attention riveted to the corner booth at the back where Liam lounges, looking as cool and confident as ever in jeans and a charcoal-gray pullover with the sleeves pushed up to his elbows.

This isn't happening. It's not supposed to happen now,

like this. I'm no more certain now than when I left Denver if he's good for me and me for him. Not when he could be the hunter and I the prey.

And yet I feel no urge to run. There's only the urge to go to him, to touch him, to lose myself in him again. There's relief that he is here and I'm not alone. And my reaction should scare me. Liam is my weakness—not the strength I'd once seen him as being.

Swallowing hard, I start walking toward him, certain he will have a plan to prevent me running anyway. He tracks my approach with those intense aqua blue eyes of his, his neatly trimmed goatee somehow giving him a worldly, dangerous air, his cool stare turning hotter the closer I get to him. And terrifyingly, just as easily, my body burns in reaction, warning me that I can't touch him without losing myself in the process. That is the power he has over me and knowing this, accepting it, is my only defense.

But my plan, like the one to stay off the radar, is lost on Liam. The instant I stop at his table he angles toward me, gently shackling my wrist, pulling me to him, my bare legs pressing to his jeans-clad knees. The heat in Liam's eyes becomes downright fire, and I'm weak and aching for this man as I have never ached for another.

"How did you find me?" I demand. Somehow my hand is on his shoulder, but I don't push him away. Why don't I?

"The same way someone else will, if you keep living like this. The CB circuit is broad, and truckers like money. And damn it, Amy, what if one of them had raped you? Or worse, killed you?"

"You think I didn't worry about those things?" I demand, angry that the control I'd thought I'd had was nothing but a facade he's destroyed with his money. "I did what I had to."

"You ran when you overheard me talking to Derek. I saw the security footage. What I don't know is what you assumed our conversation meant. All I'm guilty of is trying to protect you."

"I can't trust you, Liam. I don't trust you."

"You think I'm involved in whatever you're running from, don't you?"

"I don't know what I think."

"Would I be here, in a public place with you, if I meant to hurt you? I could have waited until you were alone and cornered you."

"You weren't afraid to be seen with me in Denver."

"Exactly." He settles a hand on my hip, and it is a branding, a claiming that sets my heart racing. "Because I have nothing to hide. And you have nothing to fear from me. Not from me. I would never hurt you."

Nothing to fear from him. There are so many ways to translate that. "Liam—"

"Do you know how good it is to hear you say my name again?" His tone is rough, affected. And I'm affected by the emotion I sense in him.

"Let me go," I whisper, telling myself I mean it, but it doesn't sound convincing even to my own ears.

"What do I have to do to convince you I'm the one you should run *to*, not away from? Tell me and I'll do it."

"Nothing is going to convince me you're my hero whisking me away to safety. You put a camera in my computer."

"I didn't put the camera in the computer. I found the one your 'boss' installed."

I blink at the unexpected answer. *Found it?* "Why would you even look for a camera, if you didn't know it was there?"

"Because nothing added up about your new boss."

"You promised I could tell you what was wrong when I was ready. So either you lied about that, or you're lying about this."

"You couldn't tell me what you didn't know was a problem. I won't apologize for protecting you, Amy. Not then and not now." He softens his voice. "Run to me. Not from me. Let's get out of here before someone else finds you."

Run to him. If only it were so simple. If only I could just say yes. "And if I say no? Will you walk away?"

"Don't say no."

"If I do," I repeat, "will you let me walk away?"

"Raw and honest, baby, no matter what. So, no—not now. Not when I fear for your safety. I won't let you walk away."

"So you're telling me you came here to kidnap me."

"Call it what you want, but I'm not leaving here without you."

"Amy? Is everything okay?"

I stiffen at Katy's unexpected interruption and try to pull my hand from Liam's, but he holds on to it. "Think before you act," he orders softly. "You're already on too many people's radar."

"I know. Including yours." My lips tighten. It seems just about everyone can be bought.

"Amy," Katy snaps, now sounding more irritated than anything else.

"Liam," I say softly.

"Be careful," he says, and, with obvious hesitation, releases me.

I turn to Katy, acutely aware of Liam standing up and stepping to my side, his shoulder brushing mine. "Sorry, Katy," I manage, despite my struggle to think of anything but Liam. "I was catching up with—"

"An old friend," Liam supplies, clearly avoiding the use of his name and this hits a nerve for me. I thought he was fine with being seen with me, but he's not fine with anyone knowing who he is here?

Katy focuses on me. "We have customers, and some of yours are pretty angry. You need to get back to work."

"Actually," Liam says, dropping a stack of money on the booth table, "Amy's resigning, effective immediately." He straightens again, still standing protectively by my side as he adds, "That should pay the checks for all of her tables tonight, and leave a generous tip for you for taking over on such short notice."

Her eyes go wide at the large sum. "Oh. Well." She scoops up the cash. "No problem. Sorry to see you go, Amy, but"—she looks Liam up and down, and her lips curve—"I get it. Believe me, I do."

She turns and walks away, but I stay put, and I don't like where my mind is taking me. Liam has just paid Katy off. He paid the truckers to find me. My father lived a life filled with invaluable relics, which translated to money. I'd tried to find a connection between my father's work and Liam, and now I have it. Money.

Liam's hand settles possessively on my back, and I squeeze my eyes shut at the shiver that races down my spine, angry that I can't control my reactions to this man. "Let's get out of here, Amy," he urges.

Panic rises inside me, and I whirl on him and take several steps backward. "I'm going to get my backpack," I announce, rushing away to the sound of his soft curse.

He won't follow, I tell myself. He'll want to avoid a big scene that draws attention. He doesn't like attention, or the press that comes with it. And I won't risk the police, with nothing to truly report and no certainty their records won't somehow tell the wrong person my location. Or maybe the wrong person already knows. Maybe that wrong person is Liam.

Fighting the urge to look over my shoulder, I push open the door to the kitchen and walk past the grill.

"Hey!" George shouts after me. "Get back on the floor. We have customers."

I go straight to the coatrack and grab my bag, then turn the corner, heading to the back door. I hesitate as I reach for the latch on the industrial door, certain that Liam will be here at any moment. But there's only the sound of something frying on the grill. Why hasn't he followed me?

It can mean only one thing: He's already outside waiting on me. I flatten my hand on the cold steel, and turn to lean against the door, my mind reeling.

Why can't this be easy? Why can't I have some way of knowing whether I can trust him? But I can't think about whys right now, or how devastating it will be if he's really a part of all of this.

I have to think through getting out of here—and there really isn't a good strategy for making that happen. If Liam is outside this door, then the only escape is through the front. But what if he isn't alone? I don't think so, but what choice do I have but to try to escape?

Pressing my hand to my face, I will myself to think, think, *think*. If I get out without Liam seeing me, then what? My money is always pinned in a baggie inside my clothes, but it's not enough to buy a car and still survive. Not unless I sell the cheap Craigslist laptop I bought a month ago—and I'll never get to my room to retrieve it before Liam gets to me.

And he'll look to the highway to find me when he realizes I'm gone. I'll have to go to one of the nearby campgrounds and wait things out for a week or so before I dare try to leave. Liam will look for me, so I can't rent a cabin. He might even look in the campgrounds, but I have no other immediate ideas. I'll just . . . I'll figure it out.

Knowing I'm out of time, I shove off the door as George yells, "Hey, you. What the fuck are you doing in here?"

My pulse leaps and I yank the door open. As I burst into the cloudy, dark night, thunder rumbles overhead; the nearly vacant parking lot is illuminated only by a low-hanging moon. I hesitate, open space and a hill between me and the motel. There is nowhere to run, and I don't get a chance to try.

The door slams behind me and Liam shackles my upper arm, turning me to face him. "Running isn't working, Amy. You have to see that."

"Don't touch me," I hiss, jerking on my arm, but he easily holds it. "Let go."

"Never again, baby. Never again."

"That's right," I promise him. "Never again. You threw money at the truckers. You threw money on the table. You throw money at everything. Well, I'm not for sale, so if you're chasing after me I must mean more money to you in some way. What do I have that you want? I'll give it to you. Just let this end."

He pulls me close, his hard body against mine, my hands pressing against the muscled wall of his chest, where I feel the wildness of his heartbeat. "I don't need money, Amy. And you don't have any for me to want, anyway."

"No, but—" I stop myself before I say *my father did* and give away something he might not know.

"But what?"

I'm desperate for the truth, any truth, and I throw caution to the wind to bait him. "My father was a famous archeologist who dealt with priceless artifacts of history. That means money. Lots of money. Your adopted father, Alex, had money, too. He could have a connection to my father."

"What the hell connection could he have to your father?"

"The pyramids."

"Alex was never into them. So if this is about the pyramids, it's about me. And my interest is in improving my craft, and understanding what no one else does. It's my way of making me better. Just me, Amy. Not Alex. And neither Alex nor I need money."

Him. There it is. The real issue. I don't want this to be all about him. "Money wants more money, just like lies breed lies. I can't afford to trust you."

Tires grind over the unpaved lot and Liam turns me to the wall, pressing me against it. "You keep saying you want honesty, baby—well, here it is. I let you walk into the kitchen, hoping you'd decide to trust me and choose to come with me. But right now I don't care if you trust me or you don't. You're coming with me."

The beam of headlights hits us, then dims, and I have no doubt this car is with Liam. "Because you're kidnapping me," I accuse again.

"Because someone either wants something you have or wants you dead, Amy. I wasn't the only bidder on your location. I was just the highest—and while you were in the kitchen, I got a phone call. Someone else gave you up. We need out of here, *now.*"

Before I can even begin to digest the magnitude of his words, he grabs my hand and drags me forward, and that's when I see the car clearly for the first time. The sight of the black sedan knots my stomach, and instantly, spots swim in front of my eyes, so fast I feel the world spinning around me.

"Liam," I call desperately, digging in my heels, needing stability to fight the pain piercing my skull. "Liam, wait." A wave of nausea and more spots overwhelm me, and my legs collapse.

Liam scoops me into his arms. "I've got you."

Pain pierces my skull and I curl into the solid wall of his chest, capable only of clinging to his shirt for dear life.

"Get the door," I remotely hear him say to someone, and I want to know who, I need to know who, but I can't focus through the pain. I try to open my eyes, but it hurts too badly to even try. Clinging to Liam, I can't do anything but trust him and pray he's worthy of that trust.

"You're okay," he promises, tightening his arms around me. "Everything is going to be okay."

It's the last thing I remember before everything goes dark.

THREE

I'M SWIMMING IN DARKNESS WHEN LIAM'S promise surfaces in my mind. *Everything is going to be okay.* The words spiral through me, and suddenly I can breathe again. I inhale air and then I'm back on the porch of my family home, standing in a dark corner with Luke, the sexy, blond god of an older boy next door, who I've crushed on since he moved in four years ago.

"You shouldn't be here," I tell him, feeling nervous on the dark porch, my brother's warning about being cautious making me edgy. So what if I'd given Luke my virginity last night and it

had left me feeling pretty lost? I've been lost a lot lately, confused by some weird vibe with my family I can't escape.

"I had to see you before I left," he says, pulling me close, brushing the hair from my eye, and stepping on my bare toes.

"Ouch," I groan.

"Sorry. Sorry, Lara. Did I hurt you?"

Obviously he hurt my foot, but I know he's not talking about now. He's talking about last night. "I'm fine. It's . . . fine." A perfect eighteenth birthday present—him pounding into me, then going drinking with the boys afterward. I wish he hadn't even come home for the summer. "You didn't have to come by. I'll see you at UT Austin in two weeks anyway." I'm just not sure I want to now. "Unless you seniors are above us freshmen."

"Did I seem like I was above freshmen last night?"

He really isn't going to like my answer to that. "It's one in the morning. If my mom catches us, she'll be furious."

"She's sleeping. You said so when I called."

"I also told you not to come."

"You're upset with me."

"No, I—" Tires grind on gravel behind me, and I jump, spinning around to see a black sedan pulling into the driveway. Luke's hand settles on my waist and he leans in to whisper, "Your mom got a little something-something going on the side?"

I grind my teeth, wondering how I never noticed what an

asshole he was until last night. I'm opening my mouth to tell him so, when the front door of the house opens. Luke yanks me back into the farthest, darkest corner of the porch, and not a moment too soon. My mother appears and I'm shocked that she's fully dressed in shorts and a tank top like me, when I'm certain I saw her in a nightgown an hour before.

Holding my breath, I watch as she goes down the stairs, her flat sandals slapping against the wood. The car pulls farther up the driveway and disappears at the side of the house, and she follows it.

"I'm out of here, babe," Luke says, but I barely register his words as I rush toward the steps. He catches up to me on the grass, grabbing my arm. "What are you doing?"

"I want to know who's here."

"Lara, be real. It's the middle of the night, and your dad and brother are out of town. Who do you think it is?"

Does he know? "Who? Who is it?"

"It's a booty call."

I gape at the crass comment. "Booty call? Is that what you hoped tonight would be for you? My mother is not cheating on my father."

He snorts. "If you say so."

I shove him. "Go back to Austin, Luke." Moonlight washes over his shocked face and I head down alongside the house to squat beside a large row of neatly trimmed bushes.

Steeling myself for what could come next, telling myself that whatever this is, it's innocent, I peer down the driveway and suck in a breath. The car's lights are dimmed to a dull glow and my mother's standing at the open driver's door, yelling at whoever is inside. She never yells. Except that day I came home to tell her I'd been accepted into the University of Texas, and overheard her fighting with someone.

"You told me it wouldn't be like this," she shouts, seemingly forgetting she might be overheard. She sounds too freaked out to think logically, out of her mind with emotion.

A deep male voice says something I can't catch. I think he's being cautious about his voice carrying, though I can't say why I think that.

"You said—" my mother starts, but the man pushes out of the car, turning to press her against the car, his big, suit-clad body framing hers. My heart is racing and I want to yell at him to let her go, but I'm not sure I should. Shadows hide his profile, making it impossible for me to make out his face, and he doesn't seem familiar. He just seems like a monster.

"Don't touch me!" my mother hisses, and the man leans in low to her ear and then pulls back to look at her.

I gasp as my mother slaps his face, the bite of her palm on his cheek loud in the quiet night.

He grabs her arm, moving her with him, and then yanks open the back door of the car. His back is to me and they exchange more incoherent words before I hear him clearly order, "Get in."

And she does. Oh, God. Why is she getting into the car? I stand up as he follows her into the backseat and shuts them inside. He's going to hurt her! There's no time to call the police or my father, and I burst from behind the shrubs to help my mother—only to be yanked back behind the bushes.

"Don't," Luke warns.

I turn on him, grabbing his shirt. "Let go! I have to help her!"

"She doesn't need help. She's getting naked with that man."

"She slapped him!"

"You didn't hear his reply?"

"No. What are you talking about?" I try to jerk my arm from his grasp. "Let go. Let me go!"

"He said he'd fuck her until she apologizes. Just like last time." He grimaces.

My throat goes dry. "No. No. That can't be."

"It is. I promise you, she's going to get out of that car smiling like a well-fed cat." He grabs my hand and pulls me around the house, though I try to dig in my heels.

"Stop, Luke. Where are we going?"

"You aren't watching this. It's upsetting you. Just do what I say, and it's going to be okay."

He starts pulling me away from the side of the house and I let him. I shouldn't let him. I should do something. "Luke—"

Blackness flashes in front of my eyes. I can't see Luke. I can't see the yard or my mother or who the man is. I have to see who the man is. But it's too dark and Luke is pulling me. He keeps pulling me! No! No! No!

"No!" I jerk to a sitting position, gasping into shadows, rain hitting the window, a storm all around me, and I yank the hair clip from the back of my throbbing head. "Where am I?"

"Easy, baby," I hear, a moment before I'm pulled back into the cradle of a hard body and a car door behind me.

"Liam?" I whisper, unsure what is real—only that my cheeks are damp and there's a tangled mess of images in my mind. My mother fighting with the stranger. Liam and me fighting behind the diner.

"I'm here and you're safe," Liam assures me, swiping the dampness from my cheeks. "You blacked out for twenty damned minutes and scared the hell out of me. Is that normal? Do you always black out that long?"

"I . . . I don't know." Nothing is normal. Nothing is right. My fingers ball around his shirt, and the murky dark waters of what remains of my flashback threaten to pull me under with guilt. "If only I'd done something that night. If only I'd told someone, or . . ."

"What night? Told who what?"

I blink and close my lips. What am I doing? I can't trust him. "Nothing. A bad dream." I try to pull away from him.

His arm encircles my waist. "Talk to me, Amy. Let me help."

My hand goes to his wrist where he holds me captive, the heat of his body radiating into me, arousing me, confusing me. I'm alone without him, but I'm tired of lies. From me. To me. About my life. "You shouldn't have looked for me."

"I should have found you sooner."

"Why, Liam? There are so many whys with you, and you have yet to give me answers that makes sense."

His fingers lace into my hair. "Nothing about us made sense from the moment we met, and yet it makes perfect sense." Then his mouth comes down on mine and I tell myself to fight him, but I don't. I can't. He is sweet bliss and burning passion that steals my breath in all the right ways. The taste of him, all hot spicy demand and primitive need, makes my senses swim and I try to think, but there is only what I feel. He molds me closer to him and somehow my hand is in his hair, spiking through those long, dark strands of sexiness I've missed touching. Just as I have missed him, and this. My resistance is gone. I'm not sure I ever had any.

I sink into his kiss, twisting around to press my chest to his, burning alive in a way only he can make me burn, and he is heaven in the midst of hell. Every swipe of his tongue is liquid heat and an escape I can find nowhere else.

"I swear to you, woman," Liam vows, tearing his mouth from mine, framing my face with his hands, "from this point on, I'm going to keep you naked and in bed with me, where I know you're safe."

Emotion thickens my throat. "If only it were that simple. But we both know it's not."

"It is. It will be. I'll make it that simple." He dips his head to kiss me again, and I don't fight him. I need just a few moments of escape, a tiny promise that there's hope for us, and for some kind of peace in my life. But as his lips graze mine, that peace is shattered all too easily by the sound of a cell phone ringing in the front seat.

I go still, the realization a cold blast of ice. We aren't alone. I start to pull away from Liam.

He holds on to me. "Wait. Amy—"

"Making me feel like a prisoner isn't going to earn my trust, Liam."

He curses and lets me go. I scramble away to sit in the center of the backseat of the sedan, too much like the one in my flashback, rain pounding hard and fast on the rooftop, echoing my heartbeat. The long rows of lights and the open space tell me we're headed for a small airfield.

"We're almost there," the driver tells the caller, and his short haircut and hard tone remind me a little too much of the military types I'd seen on some of my father's security teams. Just like this car is a little too much like the one in my flashback.

Liam touches my arm and heat flashes up it, forcing me to lean on the opposite door. "Who is he, Liam? And where are we going?"

"He's someone who needs a lesson in silencing his ringer," he grumbles, scrubbing a hand through his hair. "His name is Tellar Phelps. He handles security work for me when I need him."

"Translation: you hired him to find me."

"And to protect you."

My fingers curl into my palms. "Strangers don't make me feel protected. They make me nervous. Where are we going?"

Tellar halts the car. "Nowhere if we don't move now," he informs us. "The weather's getting dicey. We have air clearance, but that could change at any moment."

I don't look at him. "Where are we going, Liam?"

He pulls me to him. "We're going to get the hell out of here, before whoever else paid to find you at that diner catches up to us."

My throat goes dry. I'd forgotten this warning back at the diner. "Who?" I whisper. "Who else is trying to find me?"

"That's a good question, Amy."

"You don't know?"

"No—and don't think I haven't been trying to find out."

In that moment I am as tormented over Liam as ever. If he really doesn't know, then he's trustworthy—but he's also in danger because of me. I don't ever want him, or anyone else, hurt because of me. Not again. Not ever again. "Liam—"

Thunder clamors loudly, swallowing my words, and he grabs my hand. "Let's get out of here while we still safely can."

Safely. That's the key word in all of this. I don't know if anything about being with Liam is ever safe for him or me, but I'm not sure being without him is safe, either. Good intentions or not, I have no doubt Liam will force me onto this plane. I'm his captive. The willing part is still up for debate.

He opens the car door and I gasp at the shocking blast of cold rain that blows over us. "Sorry, baby," he murmurs, nuzzling my cheek and lacing his fingers with mine. "Let's get this over with." And then, in typical Liam style, I'm being pulled outside and into the storm with him, leaving me no time to object.

Tellar exits the vehicle as well, the rain whipping around him as he cuts around the car toward the trunk. Liam's arm wraps around my shoulders and he tugs me close to his side, sheltering me as much as he can. Protecting me, I tell myself. We rush toward a large jet that normal people couldn't afford to charter, but then, Liam is no more normal than I am. This similarity has often felt like the sparkle in a diamond otherwise too damaged to shine. It's how we connected the dots of him to me and me to him. And as the water pours off of us, I wonder which of us is truly pulling the other into the storm.

We reach the steps up to the jet and he urges me forward. A pretty fortysomething woman in a navy blue uniform and a badge greets me at the entryway and wraps me in a large towel. "Oh, you poor thing," she says, directing me through the narrow galley.

I step into a fancy cabin with a large tan leather couch on one side and several luxury seats on the other. "Head to the back to the second cabin area past the curtain," Liam directs, handing me another towel the flight attendant must have given him. "Buckle in. I'll be right there."

Liam turns away from me and I jump as the cabin door slams shut. I'm so damned tired of always being nervous and twitchy.

Turning, I find Liam turned away from me, one hand on a seat. Tellar is sauntering down the hallway, toweling his buzz-cut hair. His wet T-shirt and jeans hug a long and leanly muscled body, and his face is handsomely carved. I study him, expecting a pinch of recognition. I find none, but the jagged scar down his jawline tells me he's lived through hell.

His gaze lifts abruptly and meets mine, and I hold his stare. I've changed these past few weeks. I'm on a mission to take my life back, and I'm done with hiding. And what I see in his expression isn't intimidation or malice—it's concern.

Liam must see it as well, because he turns to face me, sweeping away the wet strands of hair on his forehead. "You okay?" he asks, moving toward me, his hands coming down on my shoulders. The engines roar to life but I don't move, captured by his stare, a mix of burning fire and freezing ice. Worry. Sincerity. Possessiveness. Like I am his to protect, and no one will touch me unless he lets them. And when I walked onto this plane, I made sure it's his choice.

FOUR

I STAND WITH MY BACK TO the curtain and the back cabin it covers, Liam's big body caging me . . . protecting me? It's what I want to believe. It's what some part of me needs to believe. We stare at each other, rain humming a song against the steel plane, a current of energy pulsing around us. It's power. His power. My lack of it. This is what everything in my life has come down to: the control everyone else has that I don't. The control Liam possesses as easily as he does his next breath. And staring into his piercing aqua eyes, I think that no matter how I try to stop it from happening, I am possessed. He possesses me.

A shiver goes through me, one part chill from my wet clothes and hair, one part the impact of this man standing before me. What looks and feels like real concern seeps into Liam's expression and he begins rubbing my arms, breaking the mesmerizing spell of questions that never seem to have answers. "I'll get you a blanket."

He starts to turn away and I grab his arm, silently willing him to wait. "I need to know where we're going, Liam." My lips tighten. "I need to know where you're taking me."

His head dips intimately lower, his hand caressing my head, his cheek near mine. "You were right the first time, Amy. Where *we're* going."

I fight through the warmth his soft, velvety promise creates in me. "By your choice."

"I want it to be yours."

"Until I don't choose what you want me to."

A turbulent look flickers over his handsome face. "If you mean that I won't let you choose to hitchhike across the country and end up dead, then you're right. No more, and never again. I've made that decision for you."

"Mr. Stone," says the flight attendant, urgency in her tone.

Reluctance is etched in his face as he glances over his shoulder.

"The weather reports show another system moving through. If we leave now, we have a path to bypass it."

"We'll sit down and buckle up." He turns back to me. "We need to—"

"Where, Liam?" I bite out, fighting a rising sense of claustrophobia that has me ready to bolt for the door that is already shut. "Where are we going?"

His hands come lightly down on my shoulders, yet they're somehow heavy at the same time. "Where I can protect you."

"Which is where?"

"My home."

Adrenaline surges through me. "New York," I choke out.

"Yes," he confirms tightly. "New York."

"No." I shake my head. "I can't go back there. I left for a reason."

"No one will ever know you're there."

No one will ever know. His words make my stomach knot. I could disappear tomorrow and no one would miss me.

"Mr. Stone," the attendant calls. "I must insist you sit."

I need off this plane. I try to step around Liam, and talk to the attendant, though I have no clue what to say or if it will matter. Liam seems to anticipate the move, shackling my waist with one arm, and molding me to his hard, wet body.

"Let go," I order tightly, willing away the heat stirring low in my belly at his nearness.

"We're going to sit down now, Amy."

"I don't want to—"

He yanks open the curtain and, using his larger size, walks me into an identical cabin behind us, then all but physically lifts me and sets me down in a seat. His hands go down on the arms of my seat, his arms caging me, and the engines churn to life.

We glare at each other, and I both loathe and revel in the way his heated, angry stare burns through me like a brand.

It's unsettling to be this drawn to him beyond reason when I'm this at his mercy. "There's a reason I left New York," I grind out through my teeth. "Were you part of that reason, Liam?"

Emotion flashes in his eyes, something I can't name but find I want to understand. And it's that something else that jabs at my heart, like I hurt him. Did I hurt him? I don't know how to react or how to handle any of this. "Liam—"

"I'm doing what I have to do to keep you safe. We're going to New York. End of discussion." He grabs my seat belt and latches it. "Don't make me tie you up—because if that's what it takes to keep you here, I will."

Tie me up? I swallow hard against the emotion vibrating

in his voice. The plane starts to move. Liam goes to the curtain and yanks it shut, then claims the seat directly in front of me, instead of beside me. His eyes meet mine and I don't like what I find there. I don't like the distance that I've spent nearly two months putting between us. I don't like that I think . . . I think I hurt him.

We start taxiing, and the plane is one big jerky nightmare given the impact of high winds and a promise that I'm going where it's going. Where Liam has decided I will go.

But all my worries, over control and even New York, fade into one thing. This man. Who he is, and what we are together, makes the rest irrelevant. Those things define what comes next.

Tightening my grip on the armrests, I block out the loud rush of engines and wicked shudders of the plane as we lift off, squeezing my eyes shut. I replay moments with Liam, as I have so many times before: the first time our eyes met in the airport. The moment in my apartment when he'd trapped my hands and I'd instinctively trusted him, when I had trusted no one but some invisible handler for six long years.

Just as my gut had told me to trust my handler that day in the hospital after the fire, it told me to trust Liam. And he's done nothing to hurt me, and everything to help me.

My lashes lift and he's still staring at me, watching me. I

don't like the hardness in his face that wasn't there before we sat down. He's angry and . . . hurt? I think he is.

"I'm just trying to survive, Liam," I confess. "You gave me reasons not to trust you. I just . . . I need answers."

"That's what *I* was trying to find when you got spooked and ran off."

"Well, I'm here now. Who are you in all of this?"

"Just a man who cares."

It's a perfect answer, if it comes from the right place with the right motives. "Why?"

"Every time you ask that question, I'll answer the same." He leans forward, resting his elbows on his powerful thighs. "I care. It's that simple."

"Nothing in my life is that simple."

"I am."

I laugh without humor. "We've had this discussion before. You are anything but simple or normal."

"Well then, let me make at least one thing simple for you, Amy. Anyone who wants to hurt you has to come through me first."

His vow punches me in the chest, a bittersweet, tempting promise that could easily tear away caution. "You keep answering my questions the same way, and saying all the right things. But I can't just take your word. I need . . . more."

He scrubs his jaw and then sighs. "I wanted to wait until

we were alone and you felt safe, but I can see that to ever get to that point, you need to know what I know. So here are the facts. When we get to New York, I'll show you all the documentation."

"I'm listening," I whisper, unable to find my voice, hanging by a thread over what he might confess, or where in my past he might lead me.

"I knew you were running scared," he begins, "and I didn't trust your boss. I told you that."

"Yes. You were clear on that, and I was clear when I told you not to look into my background. You were clear when you said you wouldn't. I trusted your word."

"You were terrified out of your mind. What kind of man sits back and just watches that? Your boss doesn't exist beyond paper, Amy."

"I told you not to dig."

His eyes narrow. "So you knew he wasn't real. It was a cover story."

He's too close to the real me, whoever she is, for comfort. "What matters is you broke a promise."

"But you didn't know about the camera," he continues as if I haven't spoken, adding things together far too quickly. "You couldn't have, or you wouldn't have accused me of installing it. Interestingly, your fake boss is the person who set up the Amy Bensen identity."

His statement punches me in the belly. "I don't know what you're talking about."

His eyes narrow on mine. "Yes, you do. Amy Bensen has no school pictures, no connections of any sort, and no real life. She doesn't even have fingerprints on file. But did you know that Jasmine Heights, Texas, has an abduction prevention program that fingerprints kids? You were fingerprinted in kindergarten."

I go still inside, but my hands are shaking as I curl my fingers into my palms. "What?"

"That's right, Amy. You were—or rather, Lara Brooks was—fingerprinted in kindergarten. But she supposedly died in a house fire six years ago. That's what her death certificate says. That's what your death certificate says."

I can barely breathe, hearing my real name being spoken out loud for the first time in six years—but even more at hearing that I'm officially dead. The real me didn't just leave Jasmine Heights behind. Someone buried me alive. The finality of losing all that once was and can never be again. There's nothing left. Nothing.

The shaking has turned to trembling all over. "I . . . no. I . . . no . . ." I squeeze my eyes shut, the flames flickering in my mind's eye, hearing my brother's shout. My mother's screams. "*No.*" I press my hands to my face.

Liam curses and is suddenly kneeling in front of me,

wrapping a blanket around my shoulders. "I knew I should have waited until we were safe and dry." He caresses my hair from my face. "It's going to be okay. You're not alone anymore."

"Nothing is okay," I rasp out, grabbing his shirt. "Nothing has been okay for six years."

"I know, baby. And I'm trying to change that for you."

"Were you involved? Tell me if you were involved. Good or bad or right or wrong, I have to know."

"No. God no, Amy." His hands go to the sides of my face. "I would never hurt you."

"Then tell me—*who* is making my life hell?"

He looks stunned and his hands go to my shoulders, almost as if he's steadying me. "You don't know?"

"Do you?"

"No. But I'm trying to find out. I'm going to find out."

A confusing mix of relief and disappointment fills me. "You really don't know?"

His lips thin into a grim line and he shakes his head. "No. I wish I did."

"You tried to find out?"

"Yes. Of course."

"So even with all your money and power, you have no answers."

"Not yet. But I will."

Blood rushes in my ears and my hands go to his shoulders. "No. No, if you are what you seem to be—"

"If I am what I seem to be? What do I seem to be?"

"Good. Right."

He grabs my hands and holds them between us. "I am right, Amy. Right for you. Right for us."

"Then you need to stay out of this. You don't know what you're involved in."

"Do you know anything at all, Amy? Do you have any idea what you're running from?"

"Death, Liam. I'm running from death, which is why I tried to keep you out of it. That's why I told you not to dig around. So *you* don't end up dead, too. But what did you do? You dug around. You think no one knows what you're doing? You think they won't be watching you to find me?"

"I'm not going to end up dead, and neither are you."

"My family's dead. People have died. You could die. I can't let that happen."

"You ran to protect me?"

Ashamed, I look away, fighting the sting in my eyes. "I was too weak to run to protect you."

"Amy," Liam prods gently, his finger sliding under my chin, turning my face to his.

The instant my eyes meet his, I confess. "I kept telling myself to leave, but you were . . . we were . . . I just couldn't."

"You are not weak. You've been through hell and survived, and you're going to keep surviving. We are not going to die."

"You don't—"

"I do know that. We will get through this." He unhooks my seatbelt and stands, pulling me up with him. "I won't have it any other way." And the conviction in his voice, deep in his eyes, vibrates through me, intense but somehow soothing.

"I want you to be right."

His lips quirk in that arrogant, confident way of his. "I am. And we are." He sits down and pulls me across his lap, as he had in the car.

I inhale his familiar scent deeply, and it's sweet honey pouring into the darkness of my life. Slowly my body melts into his, my lashes lower. I don't have it in me to fight him, let alone distrust him. I don't want to be alone when I can be with Liam.

As I snuggle closer to him, I can't help but wonder—if my story was a book someone was reading, would they think me naive and stupid? The very idea makes me angry, defensive even, and I do not know why when it's nothing but an invisible critic. But then, everything and everyone who has attacked me has been invisible and I find myself mentally making my own case. I was eighteen when I heard my mother being burned alive, and I was suddenly left without money and resources, barely breathing from the pain of loss myself. Maybe I should have tried harder to find answers, but most days just waking up felt like climbing mountains. Except now. In this man's arms. Would those who would judge me truly pick hitchhiking and collapsing in flashbacks while digging uselessly for answers on their own over gambling on this man's arms?

If they would, then they are not me. I am staying with Liam Stone . . . live, die, or whatever that means.

I'M HAVING THE dream again. The one where Liam is with me, holding me, making me feel safe and cared about. There's warmth and happiness, although life has taught me to expect ice and pain. Wanting the dream to last, I close my eyes tighter, savoring the sense of being warm and safe that I haven't felt much in my adult life. Inhaling, I draw in the rustic, spicy scent that tells me I'm with Liam.

I'm with Liam. My eyes pop open, and the night's events flood my mind. The diner. The car that took us to the airport. Liam pulling me onto his lap on the plane.

The hum of the engine is still present and I'm still on Liam's lap, curled into his body, his head resting on mine, his breathing slow and steady. He's asleep. And because I'm with him, I was able to sleep, too.

Trust

This is the word that comes to me. I trust him. Right or wrong, that's what he makes me feel. He has from the moment I met him. It could be instinct or stupidity. I've tried to think of it as the latter and make my own way. I went to sleep willing to live or die with Liam, and I feel the same way awake. I have been alone so very long. Too long. And the truth is, there are answers to be found and he has the resources to find them.

He shifts slightly and his arms tighten around me, as if he's afraid I'll escape. As if he's afraid this is a dream, too. He nuzzles my neck and I lean into his touch as he murmurs, "You're awake."

His voice, soft silk and deep, male sex appeal, radiates through me, and tells me this is real. He is real. And maybe, just maybe, everything I've felt for him, and with him, is real, too.

"Yes," I whisper, lifting my head. His dark hair is a finger-rumpled mess that only makes him sexier. I stroke my fingers over the dark stubble on his jaw. "And you're really here."

"Mr. Stone?"

We both look up to find the flight attendant in the doorway to the cabin. "We're preparing to land. You need to be in your own seats and we need everyone buckled up."

He doesn't move. "Oh yes," I quickly agree, scooting off Liam's lap. Or I try. He holds on to me.

"Not just yet." He glances at the flight attendant. "Consider it done."

Her lips purse, but she takes his words for the dismissal they are and departs.

Liam's fingers lace into my hair and he drags my mouth to his for a long, drugging kiss. As the landing gear descends from the belly of the plane, his lips reluctantly leave mine. "Now you can get up."

"Do I have to?"

"Yes," the flight attendant chides tartly, jerking my gaze to where she has poked her head back into the cabin. "In a seat, please."

Blood rushes to my cheeks and I scramble off of Liam's lap into the seat beside him to buckle up just as Tellar appears in the doorway.

"You must sit down," the flight attendant scolds from behind him.

Tellar lifts a hand. "I'm sitting. I'm sitting." He claims the seat in front of me. "Jeez. Women. They really can be nags."

My head prickles as a memory of my brother saying the

same thing flickers in my mind. I swallow hard and repeat what I'd told Chad so long ago. "Men. They really can be pains in the backside."

He snorts and looks at Liam. "You're right. She looks sweet, but she's feisty. I think I'd better make friends before I get my ass kicked. " He turns to me. "We haven't been formally introduced. I'm Tellar Phelps."

I don't know how to introduce myself. *I'm a dead girl named Lara? I'm a fake girl named Amy?* "Tellar's an interesting name," I say, doing the avoidance thing I do almost as well as I tell the lies I despise so much.

"*Interesting* is one way of putting it. My father was military. He and my uncles loved the whole 'Tell her you love her. Tell her she's beautiful. Tell her—' "

"What she wants to hear?" I snap without even meaning to. It just sort of happens and so does the ache in my gut that comes with the idea that he or Liam might be doing just that.

Liam laces his fingers with mine, drawing my gaze to his as he says, "I won't keep the truth from you, Amy, no matter how brutal. You have my word."

But he hadn't told me everything in Denver, and a memory smashes into me. *I can handle Amy.* Those cold words had made me sound like a puppet he controlled, and made me feel that what I'd overheard was more than Liam just snooping around. I try to jerk my hand from Liam's.

He held onto it, his eyes narrowing. "What just happened?"

"Nothing happened." But I don't want to say more and I don't want to go where these thoughts are taking me. I want to stay in the land of trust and temptation.

"Something just happened," Liam counters.

The plane jumps and shakes, and out of nowhere a wave of nausea overcomes me. I lean forward, almost doubling over, then unhook my seatbelt.

Liam's hand comes down on my back. "Amy?"

"I'm okay. I just . . . need a minute." I'm on my feet, darting to my left before he can stop me.

I make it to the bathroom without heaving, shutting the door behind me. The plane shudders again and I feel myself turn green. I hang over the tiny toilet, a metallic taste in my mouth, and I gag but nothing comes up. I can't remember the last time I ate.

"Amy?" Liam says from the hallway and I squeeze my eyes shut, angry that his caring matters to me. Angry that I've convinced myself to trust him without knowing all the facts. I'm just this stupid young girl who isn't young anymore. I can't keep using that excuse.

"Amy. Are you okay?"

"Yes," I manage, noting the urgency in his voice and looking in the mirror and seeing my ratty, horrible hair. I might not know who the girl in the mirror is anymore, but she sure looks like something the dog dragged in.

The door creaks and I turn as Liam appears, those eyes of his seeing too much. Despite the rain that has drenched us both, unlike me, he doesn't look like hell. He looks like sex and sin and the temptation I can never say no to. "You're sick to your stomach," he says, stating the obvious.

"I . . . no." Damn it—I hate the lies, and yet they flow from my mouth like water from a faucet. "It passed. I haven't eaten and . . . I'm okay."

He doesn't so much as blink, nor does he show any signs of budging to give me a chance to collect myself. He just stands there, and every second he does, he is temptation turning to double temptation. He consumes the tiny space and me with it, and he doesn't even have to try. "Is this the first time you've been sick?" he finally asks.

I know where this is headed, and I'm not ready for this conversation. Not here. Not now. "I got sick. It's done."

His lips tighten and I hold my breath knowing he's about to push, but the wheels unexpectedly hit the ground and we tumble into each other, his strong arms wrapping around me, his big body collapsing around me to hold me steady. And I lean into him, holding on as if holding on for dear life. I think maybe I am. I think . . . maybe he's my last hope. Or maybe he's my final destruction.

Soon the plane slows down to taxi in. Liam frames my face, searching my eyes. I don't know what he sees. I don't try to hide anything. He knows too much. I know too little.

His thumb strokes my jaw, my lip. "We have a lot to talk about."

I wish I could simply live in this moment, drown in the tenderness in his eyes, but instead I hear his words to Derek in my head again. *I can handle Amy.* Instantly, I stiffen, flattening my hand on his chest, intending to push him away, but like always, I do not. "Yes, Liam. Yes, we do."

His heart pounds beneath my palm. He's affected by me, and by my reaction to what he said. I believe it's because he cares about me, and I need him to deserve the trust that comes with that. So I add, "I have questions."

"So do I."

I lift my chin, making a decision in that moment I know is as right as he always feels. "I won't tell you anything you don't already know."

"Because you don't fully trust me."

"Because I can't afford to fully trust anyone."

He laces his fingers with mine. "I'm going to prove to you that I'm the exception, Amy." He tugs me close, pressing his hand to the small of my back. "But right now, I just want to remind you how good we feel together. I want you naked and in my bed, where you belong."

Heat swirls low in my belly, and I almost melt at his perfect answer that is pure seduction. Almost too perfect in a world where everything has been a lie. And I would know, since I'm the queen of lies.

FIVE

SOMEONE WANTED ME OUT OF New York.

That's what is in my mind as we exit the plane at JFK airport and enter a private wing. Passing through a lounge area we enter a main walkway, where Liam and I fall into step side by side. Any comfort from being next to him is eliminated by Tellar moving ahead of us, as if he's ready to take a bullet to protect us.

Liam wraps his arm around my shoulder and brings us thigh to thigh, his muscular torso sheltering me as if he knows that's what I need right now. And I do feel protected by him. Over the years, I've come to believe that my instincts about people and events are strong. Even as a teenager, I'd sensed there was more going on with my family than I'd understood, and I've beaten myself up a million times for doing nothing, though I still have no idea what I could have possibly done.

As we follow Tellar down the escalator, a secluded walkway comes into view, and I automatically scan for a Godzilla waiting to jump out at me. Liam takes my hand as we head toward a private exit, and I silently amend the *me* to *us*. Nothing has changed since Denver. Liam is either a danger to me, or in danger because of me. I can't win.

As we exit through a side doorway, the cold October air makes me shiver in my thin cotton waitress's uniform. And I realize it's my only possession in this world. I've lost everything again, and though I had very little, I've discovered that even something can feel like everything.

"Quickly," Liam says, ushering me toward yet another black sedan with the back door already open, and his urgency sets adrenaline rushing through me.

I climb inside the car with Liam fast behind me. As Tellar settles in behind the steering wheell, nerves hit me hard. I was told to leave here by my handler, who is now MIA. My hand goes to my throat. Oh, God—what if he died warning me?

Tellar starts the car and I shout, "Wait!" and then I turn urgently to Liam. "Coming here is a mistake. You've been asking questions about me, and you were with me in Denver. They could be watching your home. They could know we're here."

"Who is they, Amy?" Liam asks, a command to his voice, his expression grave. "Talk to me so I know what I'm dealing with."

"I told you, I don't know." I grab his hand. "Please, let's go somewhere else. Anywhere else."

His jaw sets hard. "We're here tonight. I know we're safe. We're staying." He taps Tellar's seat. "Go."

Anger surges inside me and I yank my hand from his. "So there it is. Proof that my opinion matters only when I agree with you. I'm a prisoner."

"Proof that we're sitting ducks under a streetlight, Amy, and that we have no plan beyond this one. We need a plan. I have private parking at my home, and the windows are tinted dark both in the car and my house. No one will know. And once we're at my apartment, I have the best security money can buy."

"We can't stay locked up in your apartment forever."

"And you can't keep running forever, either."

"I left everything behind and got out of New York for a reason. What part of that do you not understand?"

"And that reason was what? What spooked you that night I met you?"

I open my mouth and snap it shut as his words replay in my mind. *I can handle Amy.* The coldness of that statement bites back any confessions about my handler's existence.

"Safety," I reply honestly. "I left because New York isn't safe for me."

Liam's eyes harden and I sense his frustration. "You do know, the more you tell me, the easier it is for me to protect you, don't you?"

"I was living in New York and I left. That should tell you all you need to know."

"All that tells me is what I already knew. You need my protection."

"Why do I keep feeling like that word means captivity?"

He pulls me close, his fingers a tight vise on my arm, his body warm, hard like his voice. "Because that's what you've been in for six long years and I know you want it to end. I want it to end, too."

"I need my life back, Liam. That's true, but you taking it over isn't going to do that for me."

"That's where you're wrong, baby. Because that's exactly what I'm going to do. I'm going to get your life back, Amy—which means keeping you alive to enjoy it. Even if you hate me in the process." He settles back in his seat, his body as unyielding as his declaration.

I stare at him a moment, a million things I want to shout at him racing through my mind while I wish away Tellar. I force myself to fall back on the seat and look forward. The next few seconds of silence ripple with tension until I'm about to boil over with emotion.

"You're making me crazy, Liam," I say, twisting in my seat, pressing my hand to his chest. "If we were alone, I'd—"

"You'd what?" he challenges, tangling his fingers in my hair and dragging my mouth a breath away from his. "Because I can think of a lot of things I'd do if we were alone right now." And before I can catch my breath, his mouth slants over mine and then he is kissing me, a deep, emotional kiss that is anguish and pain, and everything I haven't said but I feel. "And being alone with you," he adds softly when his lips gently lift from mine, "can't come soon enough for me."

Nor me, I think, my breath coming out in a pant. My body is on fire, nipples aching, a low throb between my thighs. I want him to kiss me again, as much as I fear that he will and I'll forget Tellar is here.

Somehow I force myself to lower my head to Liam's chest and discover the wild thrum of his heartbeat, the proof that he's on the edge of the proverbial cliff with me.

With me. I like how that feels. I am not alone when I am with Liam.

His hand comes down on my head, a gentle but somehow seductive touch, and my lashes lower. My body relaxes into his, and for the first time in months I'm not thinking about Godzilla. I'm not thinking about lies and trust. There is just Liam.

CONSIDERING LIAM IS a brilliant architect who inherited a fortune from a brilliant architect, it's no surprise that his home is in New York's ritzy Greenwich Village and resembles a stone castle with a tower on the edge of the Hudson River. And in a city where parking is nonexistent, we enter through a double metal gate that allows us entry to private parking under the "castle."

"You designed this building, didn't you?" I ask, glancing at Liam as automatic lights flicker to life in what appears to be a four-car garage.

"It was Alex's brilliant design, which I inherited when he passed," he replies, of his father figure and mentor. "There's the main house, where I live, and a fifteen-floor building next door that houses twenty-five luxury apartments."

"Is this where he mentored you?"

"Yes. It is." The wistful sadness in his voice tells me he still misses the man who'd meant so much to him.

I wonder what it must have been like to be only thirteen, living in poverty with a single mom and an absent father, and being suddenly pulled into this world of wealth and power. "He changed your life."

"In more ways than you can possibly imagine." He takes my hand. "But I want you to."

For an instant we just stare at each other, a warm understanding spreading between us. My being here isn't about Liam holding me captive. It's about giving what you want to get in return, as he once said to me. This trip to his home is about him trusting me by inviting me into his life, where few are welcomed.

"Let's go inside," Liam urges softly.

That warm feeling seeds deeper inside me and becomes heat and fire. And hope. I feel more hope than I have felt in months. "Yes. Let's." I slide out of the car, and the nerves I've juggled for hours are now blessedly mixed with anticipation rather than fear.

The garage also holds a sleek convertible Jaguar, and I'm

somehow certain it's Liam's only car, when he could afford a fleet. And he'd flown commercial the night I'd met him, though he can obviously afford a private jet. I wonder what makes a man as powerful and wealthy as him pull back from extravagance one moment and throw money at everything the next.

My gaze lifts as a buzzer goes off and Tellar disappears through one of two doors. Liam leads me to the other, entering a code into a panel and opening the door. "Welcome to my home," he says with a flourishing wave of his hand.

I smile at the gesture and head up a short set of stucco steps to reach the grand foyer, where I blink in awe. Everything, from the intricately painted tiles beneath my feet to the high pyramid-shaped ceiling, is spectacular.

Dashing fingers through his dark hair, Liam joins me in the center of the room, where the teardrop chandelier above us glistens with tiny lights. I tilt my chin up to study it. "It's magnificent."

"Alex was big on small details, which made him exceptional at design work."

"Like you are," I comment, shifting my gaze to him.

"I can only hope to one day be as brilliant as he was."

I think of the many hours of research on Liam Stone I'd done in my time away from him and all the praise he's been given by experts. "Many people believe you already are."

"And I'd humbly submit that they are mistaken." He laces his fingers through mine and motions to the left. "Come," he says, and leads me under a magnificent stone archway.

Just inside the new room, the tiles have given way to some sort of shiny, amazing dark wood and I'm immediately in love with the cozy setting of warm brown leather couches and chairs, a fireplace, and several huge round pillars set in front of the floor-to-ceiling windows.

Liam's hand settles on my lower back. "There's a view of the Hudson River from almost every room in the house. In the daylight, it feels like you're sitting on the water."

But now there is only the inky blackness of the night sky, dotted with city lights that seem to form a triangle, like the tattoo on my handler's wrist, and at least partially resembling the one on Liam's stomach. Like the pyramids Liam is as obsessed with as my father and brother were, though despite my efforts otherwise, I've found this to be nothing but mutual interest that seems justified by their career choices.

I pull away from Liam, walking toward the stairs to stand in front of the window, and I hear my father's voice in my head. *Beneath the ground are the secrets of the universe. We just have to uncover them.* From third grade through the rest of grade school, I was homeschooled and went on digs with my family. I'd developed the passion for uncovering those secrets, and thrilled at every second of our exploration. Now, I need to uncover the secrets, not of the universe, but of why my father and the rest of my family were stolen away from me too soon.

"And I will," I whisper vehemently.

"You will what?" Liam's hands come down on my shoulders, goose bumps rising on my skin, the low, soothing sound of his voice by my ear.

I turn to face him, my back to the eternal darkness of the sky, studying his handsome face, searching his eyes for something, though I don't know what. "Find out the truth. No matter what it is, or how painful it might be."

"And I'm going to be there by your side, holding you up if you need me."

"I need a minute, Liam," Tellar says.

We turn toward our left, where he's standing in an archway.

"Now?" Liam asks.

"That would be my preference," Tellar agrees.

Liam's jaw clenches and he strokes a hand down my hair. "I'll be right back."

I watch him disappear through the doorway with Tellar. My fingers curl by my sides and it's as if I am sinking in the water beyond the window while they surf the top. Without a question, they're talking about me, and somehow I'm the outsider. I swore the day I overheard that conversation between Liam and Derek that I was taking control of my life. And standing here is not taking control. And unlike in Denver, when I had no clue if Liam and Derek truly meant to kill me, I do not fear for my life. I fear where my ignorance has kept me and where it will hold me down now.

I go toward the door and push it open, entering a kitchen with a unique two-toned round island in pale and dark blue, with pots and pans hanging from black finished cabinets above it. Male voices sound from the other side of the room and I walk toward them, seeing a finely etched black triangular table with eight black leather chairs. Around the table stand Liam, Tellar, and a tall blond man in a finely fitted suit with his back to me.

Liam's gaze lifts and finds mine. "Amy."

The man in the suit turns and his eyes go wide. "Amy!"

"What are you doing here, Derek?" I demand, tension rippling through me at the memory of that night in Denver.

The next thing I know, he grabs me and pulls me into an embrace. "Thank God you're okay! I'd never have forgiven myself for spooking you if you'd gotten hurt." He glances at Liam, who has moved to my side. "And Liam would have gone to jail for killing me, let me tell you." He releases me, his hands going to his hips. "How are you?"

"Confused," I say and hold up my hands, stepping back and bumping into the island. "And claustrophobic."

Derek takes a step backward as well, and Tellar smartly stays on the other side of the table. "You're upset."

"Of course she is," Liam bites out. "Which is why I told you not to come by tonight."

I frown at Derek. "Don't you live in Denver?"

"I have a place here, too, and I feel like crap for spooking you back in Denver."

"You didn't—Liam did. I barely knew you. I trusted him."

"Amy—" Liam begins.

I cut him off. "You're in here having a meeting about me that doesn't include me, Liam. I don't like it."

"You've been through enough for one night."

"Believe me, if I haven't broken already, I'm not going to break now."

He grimaces. "That's up for discussion."

"I'm damaged, not broken, Liam. I made it six years without you running my life. Coddling me isn't the way to make me feel safe with you again. Transparency is."

His jaw flexes. "And if you have another flashback because of something I tell you?"

"I might not like my flashbacks, but I welcome anything that makes me remember."

Liam's eyes narrow on me a moment before he steps in front of me, blocking the others from my view. "I knew you didn't know certain things," he says softly. "But you don't remember what happened?"

"No," I whisper. "Or yes. Some of it. Not all of it."

His eyes soften and he caresses my cheek. "Let's do this in the morning, when you've eaten and rested. They'll still be here."

I shake my head. "No. We're here now, and I'll rest far better knowing what you already know."

Concern etches his face. I want it to be real. It feels real. "You need to eat," he finally says. "And sleep."

"I can't eat. I can't sleep, Liam. I just want answers, Liam."

He looks like he's wrestling with himself. "You really want to do this now." It's not a question.

"I've wasted six years of my life waiting. I'm not wasting another minute I don't have to."

"Very well, then." He inhales and pushes off the counter, and Derek comes back into view, only now Tellar is standing on this side of the table as well. The two of them are staring at me. Liam is staring at me. The room shrinks and it suddenly feels like me against them, though I don't think it's really sudden at all. Maybe that's how it's been from day one.

SIX

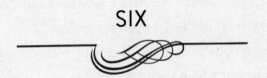

LIAM LOOKS BETWEEN TELLAR AND DEREK, and then at me. "Let's all sit down."

I don't move, and neither does Tellar, whose arms are crossed over his broad chest. His jaw is as set and hard as his razor-sharp features, his eyes angry. Is he upset with me? That makes no sense—but then, not much in my life does.

I shake my head and mimic his position, crossing my arms, and he's not the friendly jokester of earlier. "No to sitting," I say to Liam, and then to Tellar, "Tell me what's going on." I cut an accusing look at Derek. "And who are you in all of this?"

Derek scrubs his jaw and plants his hands on his lean hips. "Jesus, Amy. I hate that you obviously think I'm some bad guy. I've spent weeks picturing you raped and murdered on the side of the road somewhere because of me." He motions to Liam. "And Liam was losing his mind. Somebody had to keep his damned feet on the ground."

"Tellar, update Amy," Liam cuts in, redirecting the conversation right where I want it. "Tell her what you told us."

Tellar flicks a surprised look at Liam. "Everything?"

"Yes," Liam confirms. "Everything."

"All right, then." While his voice is soft, there's an edge to it to match his stare. "A man showed up at the diner looking for you after we left."

Shocked, though I shouldn't be considering what I'd been told earlier, I drop my arms, adrenaline surging through me. "Who was it?" *Please* let this be the moment I find out who's looking for me.

"A private eye," he says.

Not the enlightening answer I hoped for. "Hired by whom?"

His gaze moves to Liam, who gives him a nod. "He never knew who hired him. Sealed envelopes. Untraceable funds. Very James Bond-ish."

Disappointment fills me. "Do you believe him?"

"Yes," Tellar confirms. "And like most, he had a price. He was willing to do what was necessary to find out who hired him, if our price was right, and thanks to Liam, it was."

A chill races down my spine and my throat constricts. "Had?" I ask hoarsely. "Was? Why past tense?"

"He was meeting up with my man when—"

"Your man?" I interrupt and turn to Liam. "How many people are involved in this?" I ask Liam. "How many people did you tell about me?"

Liam's expression tightens. "No one is involved that I don't trust fully."

"How many?" I repeat.

"How many isn't the issue," Tellar snaps. "The issue is what happened when my man went to meet that PI."

Something in his tone raises dread in me. "What happened?"

Liam takes my hand and pulls me close. "Before we go any further, I want to reiterate that we're safe here. The windows are hurricane-proof, which also means bullet-proof."

"Bulletproof?" I choke out. "Why are you telling me this? What happened?" Liam's expression tightens, and I whirl around to face Tellar. "Oh, God. He's dead?"

"Our man's alive. The PI, however, is not. Someone

killed him, and we have to assume it was to shut him up. Who the hell is after you, Amy, and what do they want?"

"I don't know," I rasp out. "I don't know."

"You don't know? You've been running and hiding for six years and you don't even fucking know who you're running from, or why? Who would do that?"

I inhale and try to reel in the dark emotions he's stirring to life. "You don't know my story."

"I know enough."

"Enough is right, Tellar," Liam snaps, and he reaches for my hand. "Amy—"

I jerk away from Liam. "No," I hiss, and in this moment I'm that book I'd compared myself to on the plane. Tellar is reading me, judging me, pretending to know what it was like, and it's too much. It's all just . . . too much. My forehead prickles and I see the flames licking at my bedroom door. I hear Chad's command for me to jump. I hear my mother's wails of pain.

Liam says something else to me. I don't know what and I don't care. I am in my own head and in a wave of Tellar's wrath that I do not like. "Who are you to judge me, Tellar?" I demand, and with no conscious decision to act, I snap and launch myself at him, grabbing his shirt before he even blinks. "Who are you to judge me?"

"Holy hell, woman," Tellar growls, but he doesn't touch

me. I want him to touch me. I want him to give me a reason to hit him. To lash out even more. I want to hit him, though I've never wanted to hurt anyone in my entire life before.

"Who are you to judge me?" I scream again. "Who are you? Don't you think I've done enough of that myself?"

"Amy," Liam roars behind me, his strong arm loops around my waist as he pulls me off Tellar.

I lunge forward, fighting Liam, wanting back at Tellar, but Liam holds me hard against his body. "I listened to my mother's screams as she was burning alive, and I couldn't get to her," I hiss at Tellar. "My whole family died. What state of mind do you think I was in? And what resources did I have?" I jerk against Liam, but still he holds me. "Let go, damn it. Let me go!"

"Not a chance," Liam vows, his arms closing around my upper body like a vise, trapping my hands by my sides.

Tellar goes white as a sheet. "Oh, God, Amy. You were in the house?"

My fingers curl into fists, and I'm shaking so hard my teeth start to chatter. "Yes, I was in the house, Tellar. I heard every horrible scream, and there was a wall of fire between them and me. The fire spread to my room and I jumped . . ." I sob, tears falling from my eyes, running down my cheeks. "I jumped out of the window . . . when Chad . . ."

"Your brother," he says.

My brother. Just hearing that word does me in. I explode into tears and my legs just give way, and Liam is all that holds me up. He turns me into him, holding me close. "I've got you, Amy."

Clutching at his shirt, I blink through the tears. Chad's voice shouts in my ears. *Jump. Jump now.* "I shouldn't have jumped. I should never have jumped."

He frames my face in one hand, one arm wrapped around my waist, still holding me up. "Listen to me," Liam says. "Dying wouldn't solve anything. You did what you had to do. You survived."

"I survived and that's all."

"We're going to change that, baby. I promise you." He glances over my shoulder and tells Derek and Tellar, "We're done here." He tries to pick me up.

I stiffen and shove on his chest. "No. No. I can't . . . won't . . . I want to talk. I want to find who did this." I force myself to straighten. "I'm okay."

"No," Liam insists. "You are not okay." He tries to lift me into his arms. "We're done here."

"Stop." I squirm and step away, wobbly but getting stronger. "I don't want to just survive anymore. And I don't want anyone else to die."

Liam flicks a look toward Tellar and Derek. "Both of you. Get the hell out."

I growl in frustration. "Don't make my decisions, Liam. They need to stay. I want answers and they want answers. It's time to figure this out."

But Tellar and Derek walk around us.

"Stay here," I shout after them.

"They aren't staying, Amy," Liam insists, like he is the Almighty and we are all at his command.

I level him a scathing stare. "Because you can handle me on your own, right?"

"What?" His brow furrows. "What does that mean?"

The kitchen door opens and closes, and we're alone. "I heard you, Liam. I told you that. I heard it all that night in Denver. Derek was worried about my reaction to the camera, and you told him 'I can handle Amy.' Well, I've got news for you, Liam. Not only did you fail to 'handle' me back in Denver, but you're failing now, too. And that comment was what made me run, more than anything else."

He backs me against the table, his powerful thighs capturing mine, his arms caging me. Heat washes over me, confuses my senses, and I hold on to the table so I won't touch him. "I meant I'd make sure you felt safe and didn't panic." His voice is a low rasp of sandpaper. "But you're right. I failed, and we both lived through hell because of it. You far more than me, and I won't let that happen again. I will protect you with or without your consent."

"Like you own me."

"Call it what you want. But unlike that private detective, you'll be alive on the other side of this."

"People are dying, and that's my point, which you don't seem to be getting. So let me repeat what I've already asked. Who protects me from you, Liam?"

His head lowers, his breath is hot on my cheek, and there is an instant charge in the air. We are connected, he and I, and I don't know if that is good or bad. It just . . . is. "Do you think you need protection from me, Amy?" he demands. "Is that where we still are?"

Somehow, I do what I know will be my undoing. It is always my undoing with this man, and proof he is claiming the control I so desperately need. I touch him. My hand goes to his chest, and again I feel the thrum of his rapid heartbeat and it affects me. He affects me. Deeply. Passionately. Completely. "I'm just . . . I'm confused."

"That's not the answer I want."

"It's the only one I have."

"I know. I do know, and I can't even say I blame you, but that doesn't mean I like it." He shoves off the table, steps away from me, no longer touching me, leaving me cold. "We'll talk tomorrow. We're both tired. Take my bedroom. It's directly above the foyer, on the second floor. There are stairs you can't miss. I can't take you there. Not . . . now. I'll be in the spare bedroom opposite the kitchen if you need me." He starts to turn.

Desperation rises inside me. I can't be without him. I don't want to even try. I grab his arm, heat dashing up mine, our eyes colliding, torment burning in the depth of his. "Don't go," I whisper. *Don't leave me alone.* I will him to touch me, to reach for me, but he doesn't.

Arms tightly by his side, he curls his fingers into his palms. "I meant what I said. I'll force my protection on you, but I won't force me, or us, on you. And I can't be with you and not touch you."

Us. The word does funny things to my chest. "I didn't tell you not to touch me. I'm just . . ." *Raw and honest.* ". . . scared."

"I know, and it kills me to think you're afraid of me."

"That's just it. I'm not afraid of you, Liam, and maybe I should be. Probably I should be. I don't trust myself. Not when I think about everything I could have done differently pretty much my entire life."

"So if I feel right, I must be wrong." It's not a question.

"No. That's not it. I mean . . ." I take a step toward him.

He steps backward. "I can't touch you, Amy."

"I want you to touch me. I need you to touch me right now, Liam."

"I won't just touch you. I'll do anything and everything

in my power to make you remember us. To make you believe your trust in us is as real and right as I know it is."

"And that's bad, why?"

"You aren't hearing me, Amy. I've spent weeks of sleepless nights worried over you and now that you're here, I won't ask for what I want. I'll demand."

No one worries about me. No one knows I'm even alive anymore. No one I love even exists anymore. No one but him. He worries for me, and I've run from him. I think I love this man, but I can't even trust that. I'm so sick of not trusting. Emotion wells in my chest and I squeeze my eyes shut. "Please, Liam. Please demand." I step forward and I grab his shirt before he can stop me this time, as desperate, or more so, than when I'd done the same with Tellar. "Don't you get it, Liam? I want you to make the doubt go away. I want you to force away the fears. But damn it, I want you to deserve it, too. I want it to be real. I need something in this world that feels real, even if it isn't."

He doesn't move. He doesn't so much as blink. He just stares at me with heat radiating from his eyes, and I don't know what that means. What does it mean? "Or don't," I whisper, releasing his shirt. "Just don't. Just let me go, then." I rotate around and I don't even know where I intend to go. The stupid table is right behind me, and I run right into it.

Liam's hand comes down on my arm and he turns me to face him. "I'm not letting you go. Never again. I told you that." And suddenly, I am being thrown over his shoulder and his hand has found its way erotically, possessively, on my backside.

We are through the kitchen to the living room and charging up a set of stucco stairs before I can fully process that he's gone caveman on me. I can't see what is before us, only what is behind us, but I feel him shove open a door, see the dim lights flicker on. Smell the wickedly spicy scent of him everywhere around me. We are in his bedroom, and I have only a glimpse of a giant space with more floor-to-ceiling windows before I'm on top of a massive black wooden four-poster bed.

I lift myself to my elbows and Liam is on one knee, one fist planted in the mattress by my hip, his thigh pressed to mine. Heat radiates from his impossibly hooded stare and he reaches down and strokes my hair. "You want to force away the fear?"

"Yes."

"Then you have to be willing to feel it."

I swallow hard. "What does that mean?"

"Nothing goes away just because you pretend it doesn't exist."

"You think I haven't figured that out?"

"I've been where you are, and you aren't where you need to be yet. Not with me, and not with life. But you're getting there."

"I don't know what that means."

"Baby steps. You will."

"I'm tired of baby steps."

He strokes his thumb over my bottom lip, his eyes holding mine. "Then face your fears."

I make a frustrated sound. "I'm trying. You have no idea how much I want to."

He stands up and pulls me to his feet, turning me and pressing my back against one of the posts. "Do you?"

"Yes. I do."

He seems to weigh my words, and I wonder what he sees in me that I do not. "Lace your hands behind the post," he says, his voice a gentle command.

He's tied me up before, but there's a crackle of energy now that I've never felt around him. But when I look into his eyes, I feel that connection I always do, see a promise I don't have to understand. I simply want whatever he offers. I lace my fingers as he's instructed. He leans a hand on the post above me, touching me nowhere, leaving me aching for him everywhere.

"Remember what I told you before," he murmurs. "Choosing to give away control is frightening, but it's power. It's facing a fear and overcoming it. We start here tonight. We'll work toward the rest."

Which is discovering the rest of me I've rejected or lost. The parts of me that hurt in a way no one should hurt. I nod. "Yes." I want this, and him.

"Good. I may seem in control, but you are. No matter what I say or do, any time you say no, it's no. Remember that. When you make the choice, you have the power."

"Am I going to want to say no?"

"You will think you should."

"But I shouldn't?"

"You say no if you feel no, and I'll stop. You have my word."

I'm both terrified and aroused. "You're confusing me."

"I'll bet I'm about to make things crystal clear. Keep your hands where they are. Don't move."

I nod. "Yes. Okay."

His finger touches my cheek, then caresses slowly downward to my neck, and I feel the barely-there touch everywhere, inside and out. Goose bumps lift on my skin, and I nearly moan when he drags his finger over my breast and nipple. He drops his hand, and I shiver with the delicate teasing sensations that linger where he's touched, and where he hasn't touched. He leans in closer, careful not to press his body to mine when that's exactly what I burn for, then lightly, so very lightly, brushes his lips over mine. A breath later he is gone, leaving me gasping as he disappears behind me. It's all I can do not to turn to watch him.

My head dips as I inhale, trying to calm my raging hormones, and I can see only the finely woven rug on the dark wood beneath my feet. The room is silent but for a clock ticking nearby, and the rasp of my breathing. I can't hear Liam or see him, and I can't take it. I need to know where he is.

My gaze lifts and goes to the oval mirror in front of me on top of a massive black wood dresser. I suck in a breath at the drenched rat in the cheap pink waitress dress staring back at me. I don't like how she's not me, and yet she is *so* me, or how the image pulls me from the escape I crave and throws me back into reality.

A drawer opens behind me, soft yet somehow loud in the near-silence. I welcome the way it shifts my focus back to anticipation.

Then Liam's reflection appears in the mirror with mine

and I can see what I would not otherwise. Him. His chest is bare, his clothes are gone, but I'm the one who is naked, stripped of my many emotional walls by this man who moves me so deeply. The man who tells me to invite fear, so I do. I invite whatever it is he is to me, and I am to him. He reaches around me and flattens his hands on my stomach, a silk sash dangling from his hand, his eyes meeting mine in the mirror. "I'm going to tie you up now, Amy."

I wait for the fear I'm supposed to invite, but there is none. There's just anticipation, and the ache between my thighs, the heaviness of my breasts. I think about what he said to me, about what I need from him. What he needs from me. "You like tying me up."

His eyes meet mine in the mirror. "I like what it represents."

"Which is what?" I ask.

He ties my hands, wrapping them gently but firmly, then walks in front of me, one hand on my waist, the other dragging through my hair and tilting my mouth to his. "Which is what, Amy?" he asks, expecting me to answer my own question.

"Trust," I whisper, wishing his mouth on mine.

"That's right," he says, his breath whispering over my cheek, my lips, teasing me with a kiss that is yet to happen. "Trust."

And when I think he'll finally kiss me, he steps back and walks toward the dresser, giving me his back. I know then that he planned where I'm standing, with the mirror. Everything Liam does is calculated. Controlled. I think this quality is a drug for me; it's everything I wish I could be and can't. I envy it in him, admire it. Find it sexy.

I forget my hands are tied and tug on the silk. If I'm supposed to be afraid, it's not working. And why do I still have my clothes on? I really want the ugly pink uniform off my body, and him next to me.

He steps to the center of the dresser, directly in front of the mirror, and I expect him to look at me, but he doesn't. His head lowers, the dark thick waves of hair blocking my view of his expression. I can almost hear him thinking, debating, and I want to know what and why. I watch the mirror; wait with a hitched breath for his eyes to lift. When his eyes lift and collide with mine, the connection sizzles through me. Any hesitation he'd had is gone. I see the determination, the control, in his eyes, and I wonder if those things had been there only moments before.

He reaches down and pulls out a drawer. I can't see what is inside; I'm not supposed to see. The not-knowing is part of his control. Part of the anticipation and the tease he intends. Seconds tick by and I can barely stand the waiting until finally, he turns and faces me. My gaze drops, seeking that delicious pi tattoo that's so alluring, traveling down his abdomen to the thick jut of his erection, before it hits me that he's holding something. My gaze shoots back to his hands and shock rolls through me, my breath lodging in my throat.

He's holding a gold dagger.

SEVEN

LIAM STARTS WALKING TOWARD ME AND I have to force myself to breathe. The dagger is sheathed in an intricately designed casing, no blade exposed. Maybe it's not even a real dagger. It can't be real.

He stops in front of me and holds it up. "Scared?"

I wait a moment, expecting the fear to come, but it doesn't. "What are you doing, Liam?"

He presses his hand above me and rests the cold gold between my breasts. "Are you scared?" he demands.

"I should be."

"But you're not?"

I wait for the fear again, but there's only liquid heat spreading low in my limbs. I like dominant Liam. I like him a lot, and I'm not sure what that says about me. "No," I whisper. "I told you, I seem to be confused."

He unsheathes the blade. "Now are you afraid?"

I study the sharp edges, so able to cause pain, and then meet his eyes, feeling the jolt of awareness Liam so easily creates in me. Instantly, I am consumed by heat, desire . . . passion. I do not see malice. "No. I'm not afraid."

He brings the blade to the top of my uniform and pops off a button. Then another, and I can tell how careful he is not to touch my skin. I can see how much he doesn't want to hurt me. His gaze lifts to mine, a challenge in its depths. "Say the word and I'll untie you."

My voice is steady, sure. "I'd rather you undress me."

His eyes narrow, and before I know what's happening, he's yanking the blade all the way down the front of my uniform, splitting it straight down the middle. My heart is thundering in my chest as he slices the center of my bra and exposes my breasts.

He stands there staring down at me, tall and dark, lethally sexy. His gaze rakes hotly over my exposed breasts, a caress I feel in every part of me, then it lifts to mine. "This," he says, sheathing the dagger, "was to make damn sure you never wear that piece of shit uniform ever again." He tosses the dagger onto the bed and then reaches down and yanks my panties off.

I jerk at the unexpected action and already one of his hands curves around my backside, the other caressing up my bare back to mold me close, my naked breasts nestled against his chest.

"You," he says, his voice low, gravelly, "are the talented daughter of one of the most brilliant archeologists to ever live, not a waitress at a truck stop."

My chest tightens and frustratingly, my eyes prickle. "Damn you, Liam. She isn't a part of this. She's dead. You told me so."

"You're still his daughter. And whoever the hell they are, they can't take that from you. Any more than I'm letting them take you from me."

His words both carve me open and fill some hole deep in my soul. An eruption is coming, a vicious, intense . . . "Liam—"

He leans in and finally his lips brush mine, a soft, teasing caress. "Say my name again."

"Liam," I whisper more urgently, but not because he's told me to. Because there is a storm brewing inside me that he's set fire to, and I can't live through it tied to this post. "Liam, I—"

His hand slips to my face, his lips covering mine, his tongue licking into my mouth in a velvety hot caress, followed by another.

Yes. Make it all go away. This is what I need. The escape.

"I've missed how you taste," he murmurs, his lips trailing over my cheek, my jaw, to my neck. "All of you."

Tension coils inside me, part arousal, part storm, and I moan, tugging on my bound wrists. Panic rises inside me. I don't like feeling trapped. Not now. Not tonight and in this moment. "Untie me," I whisper.

He flicks me a look, stroking my nipple and sending a wave of sensation colliding with my erupting emotions. "Not yet."

"Liam, untie me!"

Leaning back to inspect me, his expression is stunned, in obvious confusion, and I try to explain what I barely understand. "I need . . . I just need to be untied. I need to be untied *now*."

He reaches behind me and releases me. The minute I'm free, I wrap my arms around his neck and my fingers are in his hair. "And I need you to hold me. I need—"

"Me too, baby," he replies, his voice low, gravelly "Me too." His mouth comes down on mine and he is kissing me, sweet, wonderful, passionate kisses. And somehow in this moment there's both wild heat and a peaceful sense of rightness.

I press into Liam, trying to get closer, to be lost in him and us. And I am. Touching him, tasting him, wrapped in the warm male scent of him, to the point that I barely know how I end up on the bed, on my back. There's just him on top of me, the thick ridge of his erection pressing between my thighs, and me aching for him to be inside me.

I lift my leg, pressing my foot into his lower back, arching into him. "Liam," I whisper, desperate to have him inside me.

His hand slips under my backside, cradling my body. "I'm the one who should be scared," he whispers, stroking my cheek, dragging his fingers down my neck, caressing my shoulder, and then cradling my breast in his palm. "I can't lose you."

"You won't."

"I almost did."

"But I'm here now."

"And you have no idea how much I want to lock you away and throw away the key until I destroy every asshole who ever hurt you." He presses inside me, and for a fleeting moment I think about the condom we don't have, the pills I haven't taken for fear I'm already pregnant. But I don't resist. I don't fear. I'm pregnant. I know it. I feel it.

He knows it, too—or maybe he thinks I'm still taking the pill. I lose the thought when Liam drives deep inside me, until he can go no farther. We stay there, savoring the moment, anticipating the next. The sound of our breathing fills the air, melding together. Seconds pass and I hear the clock ticking, building tension.

Taking me with him, Liam rolls to his back, pulling me over his hips, his hand in my hair. "The many flavors of control," he whispers. "Now you're on top. You decide how fast or slow we go." His voice roughens. "How deep I get."

The words radiate through me, evocative, erotic, and so much more than sex. One of us shifts on the mattress. Him, maybe me. The dagger has somehow ended up pressed to the side of my hand, driving home his message. No matter how dominant he might come off, he's willing to share control.

Emotion wells in my chest, and I press my palm to his face. "I'm glad you found me." I lean in and kiss him, silently telling him what I still don't feel ready to say out loud. I am his. I have been from the moment I first met him.

His hand goes to the back of my head, but he doesn't move, and I know he's waiting for me. He's giving me that control he's promised. Part of me wants to roll back over and tell him to take it, and me—the part of me that feels she's been alone forever and just wants someone to take care of her. But another part of me is ready to own my life, in a way that makes that decision no longer an option. The fact that Liam understands I have to embrace who I am, and where I'm going, matters to me more than he knows.

I lick into his mouth, a soft caress of my tongue against his, and the moan that rumbles low in his chest is so sexy, so utterly arousing, that I squeeze my thighs together and begin to move. Our lips part and for a few moments I stay there, my breath lingering with his, the dark springy hair of his chest teasing my nipples, but it's not enough. I lean back, my hands resting on his shoulders, the angle shifting his cock deeper inside me.

His gaze strokes my breasts and his hands follow, thumbs teasing my nipples. I arch into the touch and he sits up, driving himself deeper inside me, one arm wrapping around my waist, one hand cupping my breast. Our foreheads come together, our breaths mingling, connecting us fully. It's a perfect moment—me on top, but sheltered in the cocoon of his strong arms. Safe enough to let go, to experience what I am with this man.

He kisses me, a seductive, feather-light touch with a tiny hint of tongue, then drags his lips over my jaw, down my neck, to find my nipple, licking, then suckling deeply. My sex clenches around the thick pulse of his cock and I wrap my arms around his neck, tangling my fingers in his hair.

Then something shifts, and we're no longer soft and gentle. We're kissing feverishly, moving together, a wild, frenzied rush of rocking until he falls back onto the mattress, or maybe I push him. My hands are on his shoulders and I'm driving against him, unable to get enough, to ever get enough. He's watching me, his eyes riveted on my every move, every expression on my face; his scorching gaze burning me alive, devouring my breasts. Trying to take him deeper, I arch my back, move my hands to his waist, my long hair draping my face, and my gaze lands on the pi tattoo with the inverted triangle. I swallow hard and go still, my fingers splaying over artwork so like the one on my handler's wrist, and yet so unlike it—and for a moment, I feel what I have yet to feel. Fear. I feel fear and I don't know why. Everything around me seems to go black, and I can hear my own breathing. I can hear the clock.

"Amy?" Liam whispers, and my gaze jerks to his. The concern, the deep affection in his stare, tears through me. "What—" he starts, but I don't want him to speak.

I lean in and press my mouth to his, telling myself that two completely different triangles aren't the same symbol. His strong arm wraps around my waist again, and I'm where I belong. The tattoo means nothing. He means everything. Tangling my fingers into his hair, I slant my mouth over his and kiss him like I've never kissed him before. I ride him like

I've never ridden him. I take him. I make him mine, like I've never dared with another man, like I could with no other man. And I drive us to the point where we're shaking, orgasming together, my sex clenching his shaft until we melt together in utter, complete satisfaction.

Boneless, I come back to the world draped on top of him. I don't want to move. I don't want this to end, and I think he doesn't, either.

Liam finally shifts us, settling me on the mattress beside him, caressing my cheek. "I'll be right back." When he moves away I fight the ridiculous urge to reach for him and pull him back, as if he'll be gone forever.

Resting my weight on my elbows, I watch him walk in all his masculine glory toward a doorway to my left that I think is a bathroom. As he disappears into the other room, my gaze shifts to the twinkling city lights in the night sky. I have this odd sense of dreaming, and I don't want to wake up. It hardly feels real that in only a few short hours, I've gone from a roadside dump to this amazing place with Liam.

The stickiness between my legs finally invades my peaceful moment. We didn't use a condom, and I inhale at the thought, laying my hand on my belly, admitting I haven't repeated the pregnancy test for a reason. I know I'm pregnant, and I wasn't ready to deal with what that means. I'm having a baby. Liam's baby.

And now it's not just vengeance and my life that I'm fighting for. I can't fail at finding answers and solutions. That's not an option. I won't lose someone else I love.

The mattress shifts, and I'm surprised that Liam has returned to the room without my even noticing. He gently nestles a towel between my legs, and heat floods my cheeks as he cleans me up before he tosses it at a laundry hamper.

I let my head rest on the mattress, staring at the ceiling rather than Liam. Again I think about how I'm naked beyond the absence of clothes with this man in so many ways. He lies on his side, propped on one elbow, and gently places his hand on my belly. I instantly turn and face him, holding his hand in mine, resting my head on the arm I've curled under me.

"You weren't afraid," he comments.

"No. I wasn't."

"Because your instincts told you I wouldn't hurt you."

I nod. "That's right."

His hand goes to my hip and he pulls me closer. "And I won't. Ever. You were right. Human nature is to survive, and that's what our instincts are for. When our adrenaline is pumping and we have to make a choice, we know what's right. We act, and we can't look back. We can't regret." He pauses, and my breath stops in anticipation of what he'll say. "You had to jump."

Emotions jackknife through me and I try to escape, jerking backward. Liam's leg wraps around mine and I shove on his chest. "Let go."

He shakes his head. "Never again and I'll repeat that until you remember it. You couldn't have saved them, any more than I could have saved my mother, or Alex."

"You don't know. You weren't there."

"No, I wasn't. But I know there are things that are out of our control—and if we let them eat us alive, they'll destroy us. I've lived it, baby. In your case, you need answers, and you need to place blame—but not on yourself." He lowers his forehead to mine. "We'll find out who did this to you and your family, and we'll make them pay. You have my word. But it's time for you to start healing."

"I need answers."

"We'll get them." He scoops me up and moves us higher on the bed, pulling up the blankets. I let him settle us beneath the silky sheet, the soft mattress sweet bliss to my exhausted body. "Let's sleep. Tomorrow we'll come up with a plan. Together." He presses a button on the headboard and the lights dim, then he curls against me, wrapping his body around mine.

My eyes close. *Together.* I could get used to that word. And I relax into him, truly relax, for the first time in months.

I WAKE TO the ticking of a clock and blink into sunlight, my eyes fixing on the massive round clock with a heavy, etched black wood frame and contrasting delicate silver arms that occupies most of the wall in front of me. I've slept until nearly noon. I inhale the wonderful masculine scent that surrounds me everywhere, though Liam isn't in the bed any longer. *Trust your instincts* had been Liam's message to me last night. About him and everything. They seem to be all I have when I'd rather have facts and answers.

I sit up and marvel at the breathtaking view of the Hudson River. Liam was right; it's as if we're on the water. Then I take in the spectacular room I couldn't appreciate last night. It's simple but elegant, decorated with an expensive black wood bedroom set and several paintings of high-rise buildings that I date to the sixties. I wonder if Liam's mentor, Alex, designed them.

A pajama top is lying on the bottom of the bed and I smile and reach for it, hoping Liam's wearing the other half of this set. Sharing a set of pajamas is intimate in a way that reaches beyond sexy. It's about sharing and caring, two things I've had to eliminate in every form, even simple friendships.

Shoving aside the soft black comforter, I slip into the oversized shirt, disappointed that it smells fresh and clean, not spicy and male like Liam, but I can fix that, I decide. I make a quick dash to the room I think is the bathroom to find a sparkling black-and-white-tiled spa-worthy room with a claw-foot tub and separate shower. I find a brush and tame my tangled hair, scrub my face, and finger-brush my teeth with toothpaste I find in a drawer.

Back in the bedroom, I'm not quite ready to give up my solitary thoughts, and I find myself walking toward the view and the two cozy-looking overstuffed black leather chairs.

Shivering against a chill radiating from being this close to the glass, I grab the black throw on one of the chairs and wrap it around me. I'm about to sit down when my gaze catches on the dagger on the small table between the chairs.

I stare down at it, struck by the jewels and markings on the sheath and handle that I'd missed the night before. The dagger is Egyptian, and I'm certain this is from his time spent at the pyramids. This is a part of my past, as well—and finally I can talk to Liam about it. The thought is liberating.

Frowning though, I stare down at the dagger, and the oddity of it being here on the table by the window, when I know it was in the bed with us, hits me. Wondering when Liam had brought it here to the table, when I know it was in the bed with us.

I turn and face the bed and it hits me that I've barely slept in months and yet Liam stood here, holding a dagger in his hand, and I snoozed right through it. I'm reminded of how I'd slept so well that first night he'd stayed with me in Denver and I can come to only one conclusion. My subconscious mind trusts him completely: when I'm asleep. When I'm tied up and he's holding a dagger to my skin. So why, then, do I still wonder about his money and pyramids? And why, why, why, did I feel that instant of fear while staring at his tattoo?

EIGHT

I REACH FOR THE DAGGER, and I'm gauging its weight in my hand when Liam's deep baritone voice says, "Replica."

The very word I was thinking. My gaze lifts to find him leaning against the doorjamb wearing only the pajama bottoms to match my top, and my reaction is purely instinct, that of a primal kind. He is beautiful, this man, power and sex radiating off of him.

"Yes," I agree, my voice hoarse. "I thought so."

He pushes off the doorjamb, his dark hair a finger-rumpled mess that's even sexier because it's my fingers that made it that way, and he starts walking toward me. My eyes seek out and find his pi tattoo, tracing the inverted triangle beneath it that's filled with numbers, and there's not even a sliver of fear. All I feel is my desire to shove him down on the bed, crawl on top of him, and lick the darn thing again.

"How old?" he asks, stopping in front of me, his hand closing over the dagger.

I blink up at him, and he's just so damned masculine and beautiful that my mouth has gone dry and my brain seems to have stopped functioning. His lips quirk and I'm certain he knows how easily he affects me, but I don't care. "How old is the dagger, Amy?"

"Oh. The dagger. About a century."

Those sensual, punishing, pleasing lips of his curve. "Right on the mark. But then, you are your father's daughter."

It's painful to hear those words, but also liberating, powerful. I no longer have to pretend to be what I'm not with Liam. "Yes. Yes, I am."

He pulls me closer, our hands and the dagger between us, our knees touching. "Why were you holding it?"

"Why did you bring the dagger over here while I was sleeping?"

His mood shifts subtly, his lashes lowering before they

lift. "A walk down memory lane," he confesses. "Alex collected daggers from all over the world. I bought it for him while I was in Egypt, but never got a chance to give it to him. I keep it close, like I do his memory."

My heart squeezes for him, my hand flattening on his bare chest, the warmth of his body seeping into my palm the way he has seeped into my soul, my heart. "You were living that regret this morning."

He shakes his head. "I was reminding myself that regret is a disservice to those we love and who love us. It leaves no room for celebrating their lives and the memories we have with them." He leans in, pressing his cheek to mine, his hand tightening over mine and the dagger. "And last night is quite the memory."

I lean into him and close my eyes, seduced by this growing bond that defies the time and space we've had, and even the reason it exists. Deep down, I've never questioned us. This is real. We are real.

The doorbell rings and Liam groans, pressing his forehead to mine. "That will be the breakfast I ordered, which is very poorly timed." He brushes my hair over my shoulder. "I'll meet you in the kitchen. We'll eat and then I'll give you a tour of your new home."

He walks away, leaving me staring after him, processing what he's said—and what it means for me, and us. He wants me here. I want to be here, but it isn't that simple for me, no matter how much I wish it was.

I launch into action, rushing down to the foyer and crossing the living room with barely a glance at the gorgeous view out of the window. In the kitchen, past the island, I find Liam setting plates on the table.

"This isn't my home," I blurt.

He stills for a moment, a fork in his hand, before setting it down very precisely on the table and leaning his palms on the wooden surface. "I want it to be. I hope *you* want it to be."

"My family's dead. Someone killed the PI. My being with you is like painting a bull's-eye on your forehead. I won't do that to you."

That penetrating blue gaze of his unnerves me, telling me nothing of his reaction. Finally, he moves, pulling out the chair at the end of the table. "Come sit and let's eat."

"You can't dismiss my concern. It's real."

"And we'll deal with it. After you eat." His tone has that familiar absoluteness I've come to know from overbearing, dominant, sexy Liam Stone that tells me I won't win this battle.

I sigh in resignation, my shoulders slump, and I go sit down, finding my plate piled with pancakes that smell sweet and almost spicy. My stomach rumbles with a strange mix of hunger and queasiness I didn't know was possible. How can anyone be famished and sick at the same time?

"I hope you like gingerbread," Liam comments, the intensity gone. "Evan's Café next door does breakfast all day. And since they only do these in November and December, I admit to overindulging."

"They smell wonderful. But I find it hard to believe you overindulge in anything."

That sensual mouth of his curves ever so slightly. "I have a few weaknesses. Gingerbread pancakes. Architecture." His voice deepens. "And you, Amy."

Me. *I am his weakness.* I don't let myself think of how true that might be, how dangerous I could be to him, and quickly indulge in a real treat for me. The truth. "My weaknesses would be macaroni and cheese, ancient history, and you, Liam."

His eyes blaze and he is magnificently male in that moment, a devastating work of art. He motions to the pancakes. "Try the gingerbread. I want to see what you think."

Feeling remarkably relaxed considering I'd charged in here for a confrontation, I dig in. "Mmm. Yes. Wonderful. I see why you like them."

Obviously pleased, he takes a bite. "Evan's is one of two restaurants next door. There are also several high-end clothing stores and a hair salon, as well as several medical offices, most of which have been there since I first met Alex."

"You moved in here with him after your mother passed and your father—"

"Abandoned me? Yes." His short tone says he's done with the topic, and he reaches for a glass of orange juice. I think the sugary pancakes will make the juice taste as bitter as the topic clearly is, but he gulps it down just fine. The way he has every sour note life has thrown him—and not for the first time, I envy him that control.

An odd sensation churns in my belly, and I'm not sure if it's about food, or how I've handled my life. "Any chance you have something carbonated?"

He stands up and walks to the fridge, and returns with ginger ale and a glass of ice. "My mother's cure for all stomachaches. I had the restaurant bring you a bottle."

I tilt the can to fill my glass. "They had ginger ale in stock?"

"They do now."

He had them stock it for me. I soften inside. For all the hardness on Liam's outside, he's capable of such tenderness. I take a sip of the soda and it's soothing to my stomach.

He sits down, watching me. "Good?"

I nod. "It's perfect. I thought sleep would restore me to a hundred percent, but I'm still not quite right."

"You've been through hell. Give yourself time. When we get done eating, I thought I'd show you the rest of Alex's dagger collection. There are some unique pieces that might interest the history lover in you."

The idea intrigues me. "I'd like that very much. Do you collect, as well?"

He leans back in his chair. "Not my thing, but Alex spent a lot of time in Asia and acquired the interest, and about seventy-five percent of his collection, while living there."

"What drew him to Asia?"

"Architecture. They like tall buildings. He wanted to master that craft."

"Like you have. Did you study in Asia, as well?"

He nods, and I feel relief at the confirmation it gives me. "Alex insisted I spend time there. He wanted me to learn from the best, and he never considered himself that—even when everyone else did." He leans forward. "But I never went to Egypt until a few years ago, and I can prove it with my passport records."

I reach for his hand and cover it. "I didn't ask."

"But you should. Knowing what you've been through, you have to suspect everyone. Just like you had to run when you heard that conversation between me and Derek. I don't want you to ever doubt me like that again."

I inhale and decide to embrace more of that honesty I've so rarely been allowed. "You have no idea how much the idea of your being the enemy crushed me."

"I'm not the enemy, and I want to be able to talk to you about Egypt, and the pyramids, and anything you want or need to talk about without creating fear and doubt in you."

"It won't. And I'd like that. I tried to block them out. I tried to block all of it out, and I think that's what led to my blackouts. I need to reconnect with my past. My family was my everything. We all traveled together until I was in high school, mostly through Egypt and Africa. I did my school-work from dig sites. Working with my father, who was passionate and absolutely brilliant, was the most amazing experience of my life."

Liam's expression softens. "I felt the same way about Alex, and the many talented people he connected me with."

"Did you travel while you were in school, like I did?"

"Some, but I spent the bulk of my time in Asia right after I graduated from college."

A sad smile touches my lips. "My mom said I was a great student. I got my work done fast and right so we could both get back in the dirt."

"If it worked so well, what changed it?"

"My father said he wanted me to have some kind of normal childhood, with a prom and all that fluffy stuff I was supposed to want. So my mother and I stayed behind while he and my brother conquered the world beyond."

"Did you enjoy the period of being a normal teenager?"

"I tried, but I always felt like a castaway. There wasn't even a museum in Jasmine Heights where my mother and I could volunteer so we could stay connected to our previous life."

Unbidden, a memory of overhearing my father talking to my mother comes to me. *You and Lara staying here is what's best.* And with it, the tingling in my scalp begins.

Liam's hand goes to my leg. "What is it?"

I look at him, suddenly aware that my elbows are on the table and my fingers are pressed to my forehead. "Nothing, I just . . ." The memory stirs again, my parents' voices in my head, surprisingly clear. "Remembering something."

"Something important?"

"My parents arguing about us staying behind."

"Your mother wasn't happy about it, either?"

"It was hard having the family separated." I shove my plate aside.

Liam inspects my half-eaten pancakes. "You should try and eat more."

"I'm not a six-foot-two man," I remind him. "I ate plenty."

He doesn't look convinced, but I'm saved when the doorbell rings.

Liam's hand slides away from my leg. "That will be Derek coming in the security entrance. He's going to have his sister shop for whatever you need. You want to make a list?"

I shake my head. "I've been living in rat trap motels and hitchhiking. I'm good with whatever."

"You're not there anymore, baby, and you never will be again. But you're right. Don't make a list. I'll tell her to spend freely and frivolously."

"Oh, good grief. I'll make a list."

He stands up. "No list. I'll handle it." He heads through the kitchen and when I stand up to follow him, spots dot my vision. I'm going down, and I'm going down soon, and I don't want to do it with Liam and Derek standing over me.

I swiftly stumble back to the bedroom and head to the bathroom and pull the door shut. Then, practiced at this, I slide down to sit against the wall so I don't fall. As memories begin to surface I shove my fingers in my hair, rubbing my tingling scalp, but I don't will away the memory this time. I *want* to remember. It's time. To my surprise, instead of blacking out, I travel back to the fight I'd overheard between my parents. It was my junior year of high school, and I was supposed to have stayed late at school, but didn't. I'd been headed to the kitchen for a snack when I heard them and stopped dead in my tracks.

You can't leave again this soon, my mother had said. I don't remember what my father said; I'm not sure I even heard. My mother sobbed. I remember that oh so well. *Is there another woman?* she'd demanded. *Is that why you won't take us with you now?*

There was movement and I couldn't tell what happened, and then I heard my father's harsh whisper. *No. My God, woman. How can you think that? There is no other woman. It's not safe for you and Lara. I'm just protecting you. Just know I'm protecting you.*

What does that mean? my mother had screamed.

The less you know, the better.

A wave of sickness overcomes me and I crawl to the toilet, certain I'm going to be ill.

A knock on the door sounds. "Amy? Are you okay?"

Surprisingly, I am. Okay, I'm not. I get sick.

The door jerks open. "Holy hell," Liam murmurs, squatting beside me.

"Go away. Go away, Liam."

"You keep saying that, and I keep giving you the same answer. Not a chance." He strokes my hair from my face and hands me a towel. "Do you want some more ginger ale?"

My parched throat screams in reply. "Yes. Yes, please."

"I'll be right back." He disappears and I sink to the floor and lie on my back, staring at the ceiling. I didn't black out.

My lips curve through the nausea. I didn't black out.

Liam curses and sets the drink on the counter, squatting down to pick me up.

"No," I object. "I need to stay here until the sickness passes."

He looks absolutely appalled, and I touch his cheek. "I'm okay." I look at the glass on the counter. "Ginger ale?"

"Right. Yes." He hands it to me and I sip, and then gulp.

He grabs the glass. "Easy. You're going to make yourself sick again."

As I start to lie back again Liam grabs a huge, fluffy towel and pushes it under me. Then, to my shock, he lays another towel beside me and lies down as well. "What are we looking at?" he asks, staring at the ceiling.

I surprise myself with a laugh. "You do have a very nice ceiling."

He takes my hand and turns his head to look at me. "Any better?"

I nod. "Yes. I'm improving."

"We need to talk about this."

"It's just stress."

"We didn't use a condom."

"I took a test and it was negative."

"When?"

I sit up. "A few weeks ago."

He moves to squat in front of me, his hands on my knees. "I'm going to have a doctor come over and see you."

"No. No more people involved with me or us, Liam. I don't want anyone else getting hurt."

"I'll take precautions."

"We're gambling with someone's life by involving them in mine."

"We're not gambling with your life, and potentially our unborn child's."

Our unborn child's. Unbidden tears well in my eyes and I look away, struggling with the idea that I'll be bringing a baby into this hell.

Liam's finger slides under my chin and he forces my gaze to his, using his thumb to stroke away a tear. "Is the idea of having my child that horrific?"

I grab his hand. "No. That's not it. You . . . we . . . I . . ." I squeeze my eyes shut. "We . . ."

"Have a lot to figure out," he supplies. "I know. And we will, but let's start with making sure you're healthy. Can you make it to the bed?"

"I'm fine now. Whatever it was, it's over." He helps me to my feet and then picks me up.

"I can walk."

"So can I." He sets me on the bed and says, "You need to rest."

"I don't want to rest. I want my computer back from my motel room, with all of my research on it."

"Tellar's man got your things from the room. They should be here this afternoon."

Relief washes over me. "Oh, thank goodness. I put weeks into that work."

"I have stacks of research we did, as well, and it's all yours to look at. Then we'll talk all of this out and get a plan together. After," he adds, stroking hair from my brow, "the doctor comes and checks you out."

I grab his hand, and I can't keep the quaver from my voice. "Everyone close to me dies, Liam. I can't lose a child."

"Don't do this to yourself. We're going to get through this. Nothing is going to happen to you or the baby. You have my word."

There is a fierceness to the way he delivers his promise, an absoluteness, and I wonder if he's trying to convince me or himself, or maybe both of us. He leans in and kisses my forehead, his lips lingering on my skin. My fingers wrap around his wrist a little too tightly, but I can't seem to help it. I have this sense he might be gone at any moment.

He molds me close, placing his hand at the center of my back, burying his face in my neck, and I know he feels what

I do. He's afraid I'll soon be gone. He draws in a breath—inhaling my smell, I think—and I do the same. I drink in his earthy, raw male scent, feeding off of it like he is my lifeline. And in that moment, we are the two lost souls I've thought us to be on many occasions, so right for each other and so devastatingly bad at the same time.

Reluctantly, it seems, he leans back and says, "I'm calling for the doctor."

I nod. "Okay."

He reaches for his phone on the nightstand and walks to the window. My attention is riveted on him, this man who could very well be the father of my child. I study his strong profile, the way he moves with grace and confidence, the way he makes everything seem easy. Except us. We are not easy, any more than we're the calm water of the Hudson River just beyond the windows. We're caught in the hurricane of turbulence, passion, and a past I can't even remember.

NINE

IN LESS THAN AN HOUR, Dr. Murphy, an attractive forty-something woman, has arrived. According to Liam, she makes her living catering to the rich and famous. Translation—she gets paid the big bucks for keeping her mouth shut. I pray the opposite doesn't apply as well.

She and I sit by the window in Liam's bedroom, and I am acutely aware of him hovering nearby. I'm also aware of Dr. Murphy's perfectly fitted navy blue suit, and her red hair braided at the nape of her neck, while I'm a blond, frizzy, just showered mess, who barely managed a few dabs of makeup. I'm also braless, thanks to Liam's overzealous dagger action, and dressed in an oversized T-shirt and Liam's sweats that I've had to roll up.

Dr. Murphy admires the water for a moment. "It's been a long time since I've seen this view." Her lips curve. "Alex and I went way back. I live next door, but there's something about the view from his room."

"Oh," I say, and my mind can go all kinds of places with that one.

She looks amused. "Yes to whatever you're thinking. I knew Alex quite well." She pulls a blood pressure device from her bag. "Let's start with some basic vitals, shall we?"

She wraps the cuff around my arm and pumps it up as Liam paces behind us. Back and forth. Back and forth. Dr. Murphy unwraps my arm. "Blood pressure is good." She stands to eye Liam. "But mine won't be if you keep pacing behind me." She points to the door. "Out."

"I'm staying," he insists.

She crosses her arms over her chest and gives him a steely stare that impressively rivals the one he returns. "You leave," she warns, "or I leave."

Liam, who's wearing jeans and a teal blue pullover that matches his stormy eyes, gives her a fierce look. "I don't like being strong-armed, Dr. Murphy."

She doesn't even try to deny that's exactly what she's

doing. "You don't have to like it. I'm the doctor, and I insist all of my patients have privacy."

Liam eyes me and I tell him, "I'm perfectly fine."

He doesn't look convinced, but says, "I'll be right outside if you need me."

Once we're alone, the doctor pulls out her stethoscope and checks my heart, then listens to my lungs and takes my temperature. "Liam tells me you're having blackouts."

"For six years, off and on. There are triggers I'm aware of, and acupuncture helps."

"Describe the blackouts."

"They're more like flashbacks to a terrible time in my life. I see spots and get pressure in my head, and then everything just goes black."

"How often?"

"I went years without any at all, but now . . . a couple a day."

She whistles. "That's not good, especially if you think you're pregnant. It limits our testing abilities and medication options."

"I've had MRIs and CAT scans. They showed nothing."

"How long ago?"

"Years."

"That's too long ago." She purses her lips. "You said they went away and came back?"

"Yes. A stress trigger set me off again. Really. I know what's wrong. I just . . . I need to know if I'm pregnant and if the blackouts can hurt the baby."

"What was the diagnosis?"

"I don't know. The doctors just tried to shove drugs down my throat."

"Did you try medications?"

"No, and I won't."

"Why?"

Because I can't risk my thinking process being impaired. "I just won't."

She reaches in her bag and pulls out a blood draw kit. "Let's take blood and run a full panel, as well as a pregnancy test."

"I need to know about the baby now."

Digging in her bag again, she produces a little plastic cup and hands it to me. "Fill it, and I have a strip test for immediate results. Let me do the blood draw first. It's Friday, and I want to get them to the lab so we have them back on Monday."

A lab. My name. "No. No lab."

"Nothing is done in your name," she says, reading my worries. "Discretion all the way."

Reluctantly, I stretch my arm out, and she wraps a rubber tube around it. "Have you seen a counselor?" she asks, readying the syringe. "In cases of post-traumatic stress disorder, which I suspect you're experiencing, talking to someone and dealing with whatever happened to you can be helpful." She glances at my arm. "Ready?"

I nod and she pokes my vein. "I'll think about it," I promise, and it's not a lie. I plan to talk to whoever I have to in order to get at the truth—just not a counselor who could be put in danger with me.

A few minutes later, Dr. Murphy does her strip test.

"Well?" I'm actually wringing my hands, I'm so on edge.

Dr. Murphy doesn't make me wait. "It's positive."

My hands go to the arms of the chair and I clutch the leather in a death grip. I pretty much half-hear everything else she says. Something about the nausea passing in another couple of weeks. She's going to get me vitamins, and she's all for acupuncture and the counseling she'd suggested. She'll call with the results of the blood work.

She squeezes my leg. "I live next door. If you need an ear or a friend—"

"Thank you. I . . . thank you."

She gives me a worried look and seems to want to say more, but just gathers her things and leaves.

I stare out at the water without really seeing it. I'm back on the porch with my brother as he says, *You can't handle the truth.* I think of the overheard fight between my parents. Then the fight between my mother and a stranger. And then the man in the black sedan. There were things happening right before my eyes, and I hadn't seen them. Or I'd ignored them. And now they're dead, and I can't bring them back.

This baby will be here before I blink and this danger can't still exist when it does. Doing nothing is what I've done for six years. I can't do nothing now. And I can't stay in the place my handler might have died warning me to leave.

I sprint across the room toward the door and down the stairs, pausing in the foyer at the sound of Liam and Dr. Murphy murmuring on the floor below.

Emotions are racing through me like an electric charge, and I can't stand still. I pass through the archway and enter the living room and sit down on the arm of a chair. Then I stand back up. I sit down again.

Liam appears under the arches and all that emotion in me balls in my chest at the sight he makes, tall and commanding, with an easy grace and power that he wears like a second skin. This is the father of my child.

I rush toward him and grab his arms. "I was told to leave New York. We have to leave New York. We have to go anywhere but here. And then I need answers. I have to make this end. I have to."

"*We*, Amy. You aren't alone anymore. And who told you to leave?"

"The same person who saved my life six years ago."

"Which is who?"

"I don't know."

His lips tighten. "Come sit down and talk to me." He seats me in a chair and squats down in front of me. "Tell me about this stranger, and why you trust this person."

I don't hesitate. We both have something to lose now, and I'm done holding back. "After the fire, I was in the hospital when I got a call. He, whoever he was, told me that I would die, too, if I didn't leave right then and meet him in the back of the hospital."

"So you did?"

"I was eighteen and in shock."

"I know, baby. I'm not judging you. Quite the opposite."

"My parents were murdered." My voice trembles. I'm trembling all over.

"Why do you say that?"

"There were weird things going on."

"What weird things?"

"I thought one or both of my parents were having affairs. And then my brother had hinted at some kind of trouble, but he told me I couldn't handle knowing the details."

"When was that?"

"The week of the fire."

He leans back on his heels. "So you met this stranger in the hospital parking lot, and then what?"

"He gave me money, passports, and written instructions. He was only with me for five minutes, then he put me in a cab and I never saw him again."

"Could you identify him?"

I shake my head. "I don't think so. He wore a hoodie, and it was dark out."

"What kind of instructions did he give you?"

"I stayed at a hotel in Austin for a few days, until I received a delivery with an airline ticket and my new identity."

"And that identity was Amy Bensen?"

"No. Right before I met you, I'd foolishly decided I was off everyone's radar and I could try to rebuild a happy life. So I'd taken a job at a museum because . . . well . . ."

"I know why. Go on."

I inhale and let it out. "The night I met you, I'd received a note that said I'd gotten myself noticed, and that I had to run again."

"How do you know the same person contacted you again?"

"Everything was handled exactly like the first time. And . . ."

"And what?"

I hesitate a moment, but I'm trusting my instincts. "The man showed me a tattoo, and told me any communication from him would have the exact same image."

"And the note did?"

"The one in New York that told me to go to Denver did, yes. But the symbol was missing from communications after that. I was also promised money for support that never came. I think something happened to him. I think he's dead, Liam. He has to be dead."

He scrubs a hand down his face. "I need to see all of the notes."

"They're with my things from the motel. I normally keep them with me, but at the diner I had no place to lock things up."

He reaches in his pocket and pulls out his phone. "Yeah, Tellar? What's the ETA on Amy's things from the motel?" He listens a moment. "I need them now. There's some stuff inside that might hold answers." He ends the call. "He's on his way."

"Thank you." I take his hand. "There are memories coming back to me. If I go back to Texas, I'll remember more."

"Absolutely not. It's too dangerous."

"I'm tired of being the hunted, Liam. I want to be the hunter. And damn it, I want to say good-bye to my family." I choke up. "I didn't even get to go to their funerals."

He cups my head. "Not now, baby. When it's safe."

"I can't wait any longer to make this end. I can't have a baby like this. I can't."

He blanches. "It's true then? You're pregnant?" His voice comes out all smoky and hoarse.

"I thought Dr. Murphy told you."

"No. Tell me. I want to hear it from you."

"Yes. I'm pregnant. We're pregnant, and that's why I—"

He kisses me, his mouth lingering on mine, emotions rolling off of him and crashing into me, and my fingers curl in his shirt as he presses his forehead to mine. "You're having my baby."

My fingers curl on his cheek. "Yes. Yes. I'm having your baby."

His hand goes to mine and he holds it, and I can almost feel a shift in him, a subtle tension that crawls between us, building and building.

"Liam?" I push away from him to search his face, catching the storm clouds an instant before he releases my hand and stands up.

For a moment he towers over me, looking devastatingly tormented, and I have to assume it's over my being pregnant.

He rubs the back of his neck and then turns away, stalking to the window, and when he gives me his back it's like he slams a door, shutting me out. Shell-shocked, I stand up, feeling like the deer in headlights he once accused me of being, uncertain of what to do. What to say.

"You're right," he says, facing me.

"Right?" My question comes out cracked, as broken as I will be if he rejects the child I'd thought he'd embrace.

"You want out of New York. You got it. We're leaving. We're going someplace far away and disappearing."

"What?" I gape. "No. Being invisible while we hunt for my hunter, that works. Disappearing isn't a solution."

"You're going as far underground as I can get you."

"Liam," I plead, in front of him by the time his name leaves my lips, my hand curled on his chest. "Let's talk about this."

"We'll talk when you're completely hidden."

"I understand why that's your first reaction to me being pregnant—but it's not the answer. We can't have a child that we hide away like some sort of animal." And that's what he wants. I see it in his eyes. "I won't let that happen."

"You having the baby and being safe doing it is what's most important right now."

"Ending this before our child becomes a target is what's most important. I want this to *end*."

"I'll end this, Amy. You and our baby will be off someplace safe when I do."

"You mean you'll take over my life, rather than helping me get control of it again myself."

The doorbell rings and he growls low in his throat, his hands coming down on my shoulders as he turns me and presses my back to the pillar. "You are my woman, carrying my child. This isn't up for negotiation. We're doing it my way." He turns and stalks across the room.

TEN

STUNNED, I STARE AFTER HIM. *His* way? Is he serious? He claims that we're in this thing together, and then issues a command like that?

This isn't even about what the right decision is. I really don't know right or wrong at this point, except in this case. Liam dictating instead of talking is absolutely wrong, and the kiss of death for our relationship if we don't deal with it, and now.

I storm through the living room, determined to stop him from answering the door, but I'm too late. By the time I make it to the foyer I can hear Tellar and Derek talking to him, and I ball my fists by my sides. I'm glad Tellar's brought my suitcase, but I wonder why Derek's here, too.

To keep myself from spouting the blistering words I have saved up for Liam alone, I turn on my heel and head back through the living area. The rumble of Liam's deep, authoritative voice behind me vibrates in my body and for once it's not soothing. I am far too tempted to say my piece regardless of who hears.

Saving everyone from a scene, at least for the moment, I detour to the kitchen. My emotional upheaval seems to be manifesting as hunger, but when I look into the fridge, it's pathetically empty. I wait a few expectant moments and when the three men don't appear, my hunt for food has me opening what turns out to be the pantry, I find a bag of Oreos, fill a glass with milk, and head to the table. Claiming the spot that puts me facing anyone who enters the kitchen, I proceed to down six cookies and all the milk without so much as a tiny churn of my stomach. Apparently the baby has a sweet tooth, which won't be good for my health or waistline. But I'm happy to get anything in my stomach that stays down.

I'm about to go for another cookie when my hope that Derek and Tellar would leave proves futile. The three men pile into the room, staring at me and my cookies, and there's enough testosterone standing in a row in front of me to make my head ready to explode. Most women would welcome these three men for many reasons, however I doubt it would be when they were stuffing their faces with food like I am now.

Avoiding eye contact with Liam, with his best interests in mind, I set my uneaten cookie on the table. If I see that arrogant "my way is king" attitude in his eyes, I want my tongue to be whiplash ready.

Then I stare up at the three men's stony faces—or rather two of them—and they at me. Seconds of silence tick by, and it's as if no one breathes; I get the distinct impression that they're all waiting for me. Maybe Liam warned them I was a torpedo ready to blow. He was right, but I've practiced restraint for way too many years to have none now.

I wave at the group. "Hi."

The instant easing of tension in the room is like a rubber band popping. All three men seem to relax, muscles stretching and shifting. Okay, correction. Two men relax. Liam is unmoving, his stare willing mine to find his, and I refuse.

"Don't mind if I do," Derek says, setting down a folder on the table, then taking the seat at the end of the table, followed by the package of cookies. He lifts my empty glass. "You didn't leave me much to wash it down with."

I study him a moment, his blond hair neatly styled, his

customary suit replaced with neatly pressed dark blue jeans and a white polo, and although I get why Liam is invested in me, I'm not certain I'm buying Derek's reasons for being here.

Liam walks to the fridge, retrieves the milk, then moves the glass in front of me and refills it, the sweetness of the act belying his ability to excel as a complete asshole. His eyes meet mine, and the connection, that damn connection, I always feel with him punches me in the chest. "Thank you," I say softly.

"I need more than cookies," Tellar complains, sitting next to Derek, kitty-corner to the right of me. "I worked up an appetite hauling all the shopping bags Derek's sister gave me to supply your closet." He snags a cookie.

"Liam told my sister to shop for you," Derek explains before I can ask. "She's an overachiever in that activity."

When normally Liam spending money on me would be a concern, it's the last thing on my mind at the moment. "You shouldn't involve her. I don't want her put in danger."

Derek snorts. "My sister going on a shopping spree is just another day of the week. She was the perfect tool to get you what you needed. Believe me, nothing looks suspicious about it, and she's not in danger."

Liam sets a duffel bag on the table in front of me, and I'm surprised by the unfamiliar item I hadn't noticed until now. My gaze lifts to his. "What is this?" I ask, and the pull between us is magnetic, or rather, more of a current dragging me under.

"Your things from your motel room."

My brows furrow and I glance at Tellar. "Why didn't you just use my suitcase?"

He frowns. "Suitcase? There was no suitcase."

"There was." Concerned about what its absence means, I start digging through the bag, finding only a few clothes and toiletries. That's it.

"Not what you expected?" Liam asks.

I shake my head and sink down into my chair. "Everything I told you about was in the room. The notes. Weeks and weeks of research into my past. It's all gone."

Liam moves the duffel off the table and settles into the chair directly across from me. "We can re-create your research from ours. Maybe we already have."

"We can't re-create the messages I told you about."

Tellar curses, scrubbing the back of his neck. "I'm sorry, Amy. My man said nothing looked disturbed, so he assumed he was the first to get there. We're tracking the PI's activity before we came in contact with him. We're hoping that leads us to answers."

"I'll take any answers I can get. And it's not your fault. I was afraid to carry the documents with me since my backpack wasn't locked up. Obviously that was a bad call."

"It's okay—" Liam begins.

"No," I correct him, my voice lifting as I continue. "It is *not* okay. Stop saying everything is okay. It is what it is and what it is, is not okay. The notes could have helped us track down my handler."

"Handler?" Liam and Tellar ask together.

I sigh. Clearly, I'm not used to communicating with other human beings. "It's what I call the stranger who helped me hide the first time."

"The one with the tattoo?" Derek asks.

I gape at Liam. "I trusted you with that information. *Just* you."

As unapologetic as ever, he doesn't so much as blink at my irritation. "His cousin works for the feds. He can run it through the government's database and see if it gets any hits."

"*If* I had the letters, he could," I say. "And now, I don't."

"Can you draw it?" Derek asks, obviously unaffected by my implication of distrust. And honestly, if I trust Liam, and he trusts them . . .

"I can," I confirm, "but I've researched it in libraries and online, and I can't find anything like it."

Derek pulls a paper and pen from the folder and slides them in my direction. "The feds operate in a whole different world of possibilities."

A glimmer of hope forms inside me, and I make a drawing of the tattoo as best I can, drawing the triangle and the odd design in the center. Inspecting my work, I flip the paper around for Derek to see. "That's pretty close."

Liam reaches across the table and drags the drawing to him, giving it a close review, and I don't miss the muscle in his jaw that jumps. His steely eyes find mine. "The only thing similar about this tattoo and mine is the triangle. There is no connection, and this means nothing to me. You know that, right?"

Shocked by his directness—though I really don't know why; this is Liam I'm dealing with—I nod. "I know."

His jaw tenses, flexes. "Do you? Because I'm not sure I'm convinced."

"I am. I know."

His attention stays fixed on me, his eyes never leaving my face. "Okay then," Tellar says, sliding the paper closer to look at it. "Means nothing to me, either."

"Ditto," Derek agrees, "but we'll see what my cuz has to say."

Liam's gaze snaps to Derek and he taps the table. "Did you bring the papers I asked you to bring?" Derek pulls a bundle of stapled documents from the folder and holds them up. Liam motions to me. "Give them to Amy."

Frowning, I accept the documents, not sure what to expect. "Travel records for me and Alex," Liam explains. "I want you to see there is no connection between us and your family."

"I . . . Liam, I didn't ask for this."

"You didn't have to—and you don't have to ask to look at the research we did on your life, either. It's your life." His expression tells me his choice of words is deliberate. "We put together a list of everyone who could be connected to you and your family, and looked for anything suspicious. There's nothing that connects the dots for us, but there might be for you."

"I hope so; I . . ." The memory of me and Luke kneeling near the bushes while I watched my mother argue with the man by the black sedan comes to me. I straighten with the impact. Luke. I need to talk to Luke.

"Amy?" Liam asks, sounding concerned.

I blink him into view, eager to share what I've remembered. "There was a boy who lived next door to me in Texas, named Luke Miller. He was with me one night when my brother and father were out of town. It was midnight and we were standing on the porch when this black sedan pulled into the driveway and then to the side of the house. My mother raced out the door and down the steps. She never saw us. We hid at the side of the house and listened as she argued with the driver."

"What were they arguing about?" Derek asks.

"I'm going to give my standard answer. I don't know. Their voices were too muffled." I inhale and force myself to admit what I don't want to be real. "But based on their body language and the emotional context of the exchange, I'm pretty sure there was something personal between them."

Liam arches a brow. "An affair?"

I hate to agree, so I shrug. I can't manage anything else.

Derek clears his throat. "At the risk of sounding insensitive, Amy, I feel like I need to say this. Statistically, my cousin would tell you to look close to home and in the bedroom when a murder takes place. I think this man is a good lead."

"I'm not denying that you could be right," I assure him. "But I'm also convinced there was something going on with my father and brother. And before you ask me how I know, I have nothing to go on but a vague warning from my brother to me, and a warning I overhead from my father to my mother about protecting us."

"Listen to your instincts, baby," Liam reminds me softly. "They haven't failed you."

"My instincts say I need to talk to Luke and find out what he saw that night. But I'm not sure how I can do that when I'm supposed to be dead."

"I can do it," Tellar offers. "I'll come up with some masterful story like being a reporter writing a story on your famous father. What do you think he might know that you don't?"

"I didn't see the man's face. Luke snuck around the driveway to leave, and it's possible he did."

"You never talked about it later?" Liam asks.

"He was home on a college break, and we pretty much parted ways that night."

"Miller," Derek repeats absently. "Miller. I remember that name." He opens a folder, scans down what appears to be a list, and his expression tightens, his discomfort palpable. "I have his information."

Dread washes over me, and Liam's tone is cautious as he asks, "What does that mean? What information?"

Derek shows Liam a piece of paper. Liam gives the document a slow inspection, his expression unreadable. Abruptly, he stands up. "Let's go upstairs and talk, Amy."

My world spins and I'm on my feet in an instant, holding on to the table for support. "He's dead, isn't he? He's dead because of me in some way."

Liam's expression is still as unreadable as a blank page, his reply nonexistent.

"Just *tell* me. Is Luke dead?"

He gives a sharp nod. "He's dead."

"When and how?"

"Six months after your house fire, he was killed in a car accident."

"And we both know it wasn't an accident." My voice trembles, and the audience of men I didn't want in the first place is suffocating. I cut around the table and rush through the kitchen, running up the foyer stairs toward the bedroom. Darkness greets me at the top and I pause, a chill slithering down my spine.

The dark, windowless tunnel of a hallway leads to parts of the house that I haven't explored, but wish I had. The unknown is not my friend. It's proven that to me over and over with the force of a sharp whip. I glance over my shoulder and wish my normally overwhelming man would appear.

My man. I think of Liam as my man.

I shake off a complicated ball of emotions and focus my attention forward, searching for the light switch I don't find. Giving up, I push open the bedroom door to my right, relieved that the massive windows and late afternoon sun cast the room in a warm glow.

Heart racing, I lean against the wall, almost expecting some stranger to come flying after me. I shove my fingers through my hair. I'm being paranoid. The house is safe. It's Luke who was not. Like everyone who steps into my path, he's dead now. He's dead and it doesn't matter I haven't talked to him for years or that he pretty much wasn't a nice person. He was young and never got the chance to become more, and I can't help but feel responsible.

At the time, hiding from danger had seemed the smart thing to do. Now, though, with the P.I. and Luke dead, and who knows who else, and while I have no idea how I would have fought this battle at the young age of eighteen with no resources, at least it would have been my life on the line, not theirs.

My hand settles on my belly, on the new life I am responsible for. Though I'm certain that returning to Texas would trigger my memories, that's no longer an option. I could end up dead, and my unborn child with me. Liam could end up dead with me.

Footsteps sound on the stairs, and I whisper "Liam" as he enters the room, stepping toward him. I am linked to this man. In all his dominating, good and bad, he matters to me. He is my heart.

His hands instantly settle at my waist. The impact of his touch is so powerful that it's frightening, how easily I could let him get away with just his silent apology in the kitchen, when his earlier behavior was too out of line to just let slide. "We have to talk, Liam."

"I was a complete asshole," he replies, cutting right to the point. "I know. But after what we just learned in that kitchen, you have to see that Texas is a death wish."

I blanch. "Are you seriously justifying being an asshole?"

"I'm not apologizing at all. I'm telling you how it is. You will not get yourself and my baby killed."

"*Our* baby, Liam. Just like *we* and *together* does not mean you treating me like property. You can call me yours when you learn the difference."

He shackles my legs with his, then shoves my hands over my head, his eyes blazing. "You're mine. No matter what name you use or where you run, you are mine."

His words whip through me, affecting me on every possible level. "I thought you weren't going there, Liam. I thought you said this wasn't what I needed right now."

"Even your neighbor is dead, baby. That opened my eyes. You're mine, and that, to me, means to protect you"—he slides his hand around my backside and molds my hips to his—"and make you scream my name as often and in as many creative ways as I can."

My thighs all but vibrate with his words. "Saying I'm yours doesn't make it so."

"No?" he challenges, his lips, his breath, teasing my cheek and mouth, his hand brushing over my chest, my nipple, and settling at the drawstring at my waist that he unties. "Are you sure about that?"

"Yes," I manage, despite the way his fingers find their

way beneath my shirt, teasing the skin there, reminding me that I'm braless, exposed.

His eyes glint with a cool arrogance that both makes me want to kick him and lick him before he says, "I'm not convinced," and proceeds to caress a path up my rib cage to my breasts.

I dig my fingers into his shoulders, fighting a moan of pure submission when his fingers find my nipples and tease, then tug, the touch as rough and erotic as his words when he'd declared me his.

He leans closer, the wicked male scent of him teasing my nostrils, his sensual mouth brushing my ear, teeth teasing the delicate lobe. "I told you once you weren't alone, and vowed to make sure you didn't forget that. Now, I'll rephrase. You aren't alone, and you're mine. If you don't know those things, I haven't been clear enough, but I will. Right here. Right now."

I squeeze my eyes shut, trying to think of a reply, but his lips, those damned perfect lips of his, distract me, caressing my neck, sending waves of sensation through me and leaving goose bumps in their wake. They find my mouth, brush it with a feather-light touch that has me balling my fingers in his shirt as he whispers, "Mine," and then drags the T-shirt I'm wearing upward. He pulls it over my head and tosses it away before I can process what's happening.

His hands go back to mine and he shackles my wrists, shoving them against the wall above me. "Leave them there until I tell you that you can move them."

"Why would I do that?" I ask, all too aware that I am bare above the waist, my breasts thrust in the air, and it's both daunting and arousing to be exposed, in ways I think he understands more than I do.

His expression is dark, his tone absolute. "It's your choice. It's always your choice."

"You said we were doing everything your way. That's not a choice."

"I said that I won't let you get yourself killed. You're right. That isn't a choice."

He surprises me by abruptly turning me to face the wall, forcing me to hold my hands braced on the solid surface to support myself. Almost instantly he shoves my pants down, and I gasp with the shock of the cool air on my backside, then nearly sigh at the blessed relief it delivers to my heated skin. He slides my sweats down my hips and goes with them, squatting at my feet, and I don't even try to stop him from removing my tennis shoes. When the job is done, when I have let him strip me bare, leaving him completely dressed, in control. He stands and arches over me, flattening his hands over mine and moving them back where he wanted them—over my head—and I have no option but to keep them there or crash into the wall. I want to crash into him. There is no denying it, and while there are many things I want to escape, he is not one of them.

The feel of his big body wrapped around me, the thick pulse of his erection resting against my backside, is too much, yet not enough. He skims down my arms, reaching around me to my naked breasts, his fingers tugging and twisting my nipples until my thighs are damp and my sex aching. Finally his hand moves lower, palms resting erotically on my backside, and he leans into me. "I think I might just tie you up in my bed and keep you there, like I threatened. You'd be mine for sure then. I could lick you, kiss you . . . punish you for denying you're mine. Maybe even spank your pretty little ass."

ELEVEN

SPANK ME? I GASP AND TRY to turn, my heart exploding in my chest, but he holds me easily, his fingers wrapping my wrists. One of his hands goes to my breast, cupping it, holding my back to his chest. "Easy, baby," he murmurs. "I won't spank you unless you ask me to."

The growly, deep quality of his voice is frighteningly arousing, considering the topic. "That's never going to happen."

"It's not about pain, baby. It's erotic pleasure and the kind of complete escape that leaves nothing but the moment. And the trust you give me because you're mine. It leaves no room for anything but you and me. You need that. We need that."

Any fear of the threat of a spanking evaporates. *Yes*, I whisper in my mind. *I need that. Take me. Make me yours.* I squeeze my eyes shut and when he turns me to face him, I open them. His eyes hold me spellbound, the air thickening around us. He presses his fists into the wall by my head and tenderness settles over his face as he adds, "But what we need more than anything, Amy, is each other. I need you, baby. I need you alive and well, in my bed and in my life. The idea of losing you is torture, but I know you aren't my property. You're the woman who changed me in ways I don't even fully understand."

We are both naked now, exposed in ways I don't believe we've ever been with anyone else. The raw honesty in his eyes, the torment and fear, the vulnerability I sense in him, speak to my soul. He speaks to my soul. And suddenly I understand the sex games, and his need to control something when everything seems to be spinning and breaking apart.

I wrap my arms around his neck. "You're right. We do need each other. I need you, Liam, but—"

"No buts." He slides his fingers around my neck, dragging my mouth to his. "Say it again. I want to hear you say it again."

My heart squeezes with the vulnerability and need beneath his masculine command. His need for me. Mine for him. "I need you, Liam."

"And that is everything to me, Amy. You are everything."

He kisses me, his tongue parting my lips, and when mine reaches for his, when that first sensual connection happens, it's as if something bursts to life between us. This isn't a kiss, but an unleashing of wild heat. We're suddenly clinging to each other, touching each other, his arms wrapping around my neck, my legs around his waist.

In an instant I'm sandwiched between him and the wall, and his pants are to his knees, his shaft pushing into the slickness of my sex. He drives into me, stretching me, filling me, burying himself deeply, completely. I pant with the feel of him inside me, our foreheads settling together—another little thing that has become familiar, a sweet bond in the middle of absolute passion.

"You aren't even undressed," I whisper.

"We'll do it in reverse next time," he promises, and I laugh. Then he lifts me off of the wall, taking all of my weight, angling my hips and his cock for a deep, hard push that has me moaning.

Clinging to his neck, I have a fleeting moment of worry about how he is holding my full weight, but it is gone with another pump of his cock, I'm lost to his sexy, guttural groans. Curling into him, burying my face in his neck, I forget everything but the way he moves, the way he grinds into me. Time stands still for the push and pull of our bodies that lands me on my back on the mattress, legs over his shoulders, and yes, oh yes, his cock is deeper inside me, and he's driving harder and harder, faster and faster.

The muscles in my sex tighten, burning with the promise of something sweet and wonderful. "Liam . . . I . . . I . . ." He leans in and kisses me, still managing to seduce me with the thick pump of his cock. All too easily, he chooses when to push me to the edge and into a waterfall of sensations so intense, the pleasure borders on pain. I grasp the blankets beneath me, trying to stay in the moment, willing it to last, but it escapes me, leaves me panting, drugged with the impact.

It is gone, but Liam is not. I come back to the world with another deep thrust of his shaft that has him shuddering from head to toe, and the intensity on his face, the primal beast he is in that moment, is the most beautiful thing I've ever seen. He collapses on top of me, completely drained yet careful not to crush me, aware of me even in his own escape.

Seconds pass and neither of us speaks; we don't need to. It is good and right between us. When he finally moves, rather than pulling out of me, Liam adjusts his pants enough to stand. I wrap myself around him without questioning his intentions.

We enter the bathroom to the flicker of automatic lights as he sets me on the counter and grabs a towel, pressing it between my legs as he pulls out of me.

His hand goes to the back of my head and he does that now familiar thing he does and rests his forehead against mine. I nestle my fingers in the soft, springy hair of his broad chest and breathe with him, a deeper intimacy blooming between us.

"About earlier tonight," he begins.

"It's okay—"

"No. It's my turn to say it's not okay." He eases back to look at me, and those sharks he claims swim around his feet are swimming in his eyes. "I was an asshole."

"You're worried, and you'd just been handed a VIP invitation to fatherhood you hadn't planned for."

"A VIP invitation to be a better man than my father, Amy."

My lips part at the unexpected answer. "Oh, Liam—"

"Hear me out, baby." His gaze flickers over my bare chest and he grabs a navy blue cotton robe from behind the door and slides it over my shoulders. "It's hard to think, let alone say what I have to say, when you're naked."

Cheeks burning, I stick my arms through the huge sleeves while he tugs the robe shut and ties it, his hands lingering on the knot at my waist.

He lets out a heavy breath. "Okay." He hesitates, then seems to push himself to confess, "When I was a kid, my father used to get drunk and beat my mother."

My eyes go wide and I open my mouth to issue words of sympathy, but I read the way he seems to wait for the bullets they would represent, and instead ask, "Did he hit you?"

"Oddly, no. But for years I was the small child hiding in the closet while he played monster. I'd shout and try to hit him, but my mother begged me to stop. I was little, only eight, and she was sure I'd be hurt. Thankfully, the SOB disappeared. That was the best thing that ever happened to my mother. Then when I was thirteen, he came back for a night and my mother let him in her bed, to wake up to a beating." His expression turns dark and haunted. "I was already six feet tall, I had listened to too many brutal attacks before, and I punched him—hard."

Pride wells inside me at his bravery as a young boy who'd been through too much, too soon in life. "What happened?" I whisper, reading his tone as a resolution.

"He left. The end. And that's where I was at today, when I said it was going to be my way. Back then I knew standing up to my father was right, and right now I know hiding you well is the answer. The only good thing he ever taught me was that I can't do nothing, Amy—and I can't ignore my own instincts."

"Nothing is exactly what I've done for the past six years, Liam."

"No. You survived and that says a lot."

"That's not enough. We've had this discussion."

"You survived until you got here, with me. Now, you can lean on me."

I shake my head. "But I can't just let you take care of me. And even if I was willing, I'm the link to all of this. I'm the problem and the solution."

His jaw sets hard. "We can't go to Texas."

"I know." My whispered acceptance is etched in the pain of loss no longer hidden deep in my soul. I clear my throat and add, "But we can't raise a child in hiding, always looking around every corner."

"I didn't say hide forever. But in the past twenty-four hours, a lot has become clear: like the willingness of whoever this is to kill anyone they see as a threat. And the fact that they appear to have ample resources of their own.

Which means we need to get underground until we figure out a fighting plan."

"That's not how you made it sound earlier."

"I'm still going to want to leave you locked away and safe."

"And—"

He kisses me. "I know. I know you can't spend your life that way. We'll figure it out."

Relief and appreciation for this man fills in my chest. "So where does that leave us now?"

"Moving just to move is dangerous. It means more people to see you, and there are more chances to be found—and that's dangerous when there's a ransom on your head. We'll stay here a few days, get our ducks in a row, and then we move."

"And go where?"

"Asia. I have connections there, and those connections, with my money, will be hard to penetrate."

Asia. My head is spinning. "What about a new passport? I can't travel as Amy Bensen anymore. Whoever's after me, whoever had that private investigator killed, must know that identity."

"I'll charter a plane and handle whatever paperwork needs to be dealt with." He grabs the lapels of my robe. "We'll end this. You have my word."

"Yes—*we*. If I'm going to another country with you, Liam, you need to mean that this time."

"I meant it every time I said it—but baby, I have my own Godzillas. I can't promise—"

"Not to be an asshole?"

"But always with good intentions."

"Hmmmm." I slide my hands under his shirt. "Well . . . good intentions gone bad always come with a price. I think you need to be spanked."

His eyes light with mischief, and I watch what's left of the darkness in his eyes fade. "You're going to spank me?"

"That's right. But you have on too many clothes."

"Never let it be said that I resisted my punishment." His lips curve and he tugs his shirt over his head. "Better?"

"Getting there."

He steps away from me, and the gleam of satisfaction in his eyes as he removes his shoes warns me *I'm* the one who's about to get spanked. I should be worried about that, but my earlier fear is gone. My gaze hungrily travels his ripped torso and lands on the tattoo peeking from his unzipped pants, and suddenly it means so much more to me than before. It has become a symbol of the little boy who had a monster for a father and lost his mother too young, but who didn't quit.

Affection fills me and I slide off the counter to wrap my

arms around him. "You had so many reasons to fail in life, yet you became such an amazing person. I'm going to fight like you did. For me and for us." I sink down to my knees in front of him, setting my hand on his tattoo. "I am infinitely yours, Liam Stone."

He pulls me to my feet, molding me close. "Say it again," he orders, his voice a raspy command.

I smile at this repeating theme. "I am infinitely yours, Liam Stone." I curl my fingers on his jaw. "Now you say it."

"You are infinitely mine."

I glower at him and he gives me a devastating smile. "Baby, I've been yours from the moment I laid eyes on you." He unties the robe. "Shall I show you? Or are you eager to continue with the punishment?"

"*Yours*, not mine."

His lips hint at a curve. "We'll see about that." He slides his pants down his legs, and there is no question that he's risen to the challenge of "showing me."

"No," I say, pulling the robe shut. "We won't." But I'm not afraid. I'm never afraid with Liam.

He steps up to me, his expression all dark promise and smoky sensuality. "Like I said. We'll see about that." He shoves the robe down my shoulders.

I catch it at my elbows. "I'm pregnant."

He arches a brow. "And that means what?"

"I'm pregnant," I repeat.

"We could ask Dr. Murphy if—"

"We are *not* asking her any such thing."

He laughs, a deep rumble of pure sex that I feel in every part of me. "Then I guess we'll just have to figure it out for ourselves, won't we?"

My sex clenches, and I'm horrified to realize how aroused this is making me. "Not now."

"I'm in no rush." He pulls my mouth to his. "I'm all about savoring you, now that you're mine. Nice and slow, baby."

And then he proceeds to convince me that his kind of slow is really, really good.

THE NEXT MORNING I stand in the massive closet, freshly showered and dressed in a new pink silk robe. Thanks to the hair products Derek's sister purchased for me, my hair is blow-dried straight and shiny. All around me are bags filled with more items, and while I'm incredibly grateful for the gifts, what really makes me smile is thinking about the way Liam declared half the closet mine before heading to the kitchen to arrange grocery delivery.

Thanks to his convincing me to stay in bed with him last night for a *Lord of the Rings* marathon, I feel rested for the first time in months. Of course, having him naked in bed beside me made my agreement fairly easy, but I'd known I was physically and emotionally at my limit, too. As a bonus, the pizza we ordered to eat in bed was not only yummy, but didn't make me sick. I almost think the sickness was more about stress and exhaustion than the pregnancy.

After arranging all my new things, I dress in a black velvet Victoria's Secret sweatsuit with stylish wedge-heeled tennis shoes. I suspect they'll soon be all that fits of this trim outfit, and I'm looking forward to a visit from Dr. Murphy on Monday to talk about my due date and general care.

Looking casually sexy in gray sweats and a red T-shirt with the pi sign on it, Liam appears in the bedroom doorway. His eyes light on me, and his genuine pleasure at having me here warms me to the core. "Let's go get you comfortable with your new home, why don't we?"

My stomach knots with his words as he leads me along with him, the real world I've spent hours hiding from striking its angry sword at me, reminding me of what I've pretended didn't exist. I'm hungry for stability, for home. But I'm still on the run, and once I leave here, I may never be back. All the more reason to enjoy every second of the here and now, I remind myself, aware in deep, gut-wrenching ways how easily tomorrow might not exist.

We walk down the long hallway that leads to several elegantly decorated bedrooms, and a library filled with architecture books and models of buildings Alex created. We spend a good hour talking about those, and then finally we enter the Dagger Room.

The long, rectangular room, the size of two giant master bedrooms, is nearly all windows. Alex's dagger collection is displayed in at least a dozen glass cases framed in gray wood, with clawfoot legs etched in intricate designs.

Liam waves me forward and I eagerly move to the first case as he explains, "You'll find them divided by region and time period. And as I mentioned, the collection is heavily influenced by Alex's Asian interests."

My eyes go wide when I see a jade-handled dagger with remnants of dirt and age on the ivory blade and I read "Shang Dynasty, ca. 1046 BCE." Stunned, I look at Liam. "This is museum-worthy."

"And now you know why I have a state-of-the-art security system."

"Yes, I do." I glance around at some of the other pieces and add, "I hope it's really as good as you say it is."

"I wouldn't have brought you here if it wasn't. We're

wired like Fort Knox, baby. Though Alex put a lifetime into this collection and I want to keep them safe, I'm not sure I enjoy them the way they should be enjoyed. I need to find a museum to donate them to."

Surprised, I turn and see the sadness in his eyes. "Are you sure you want to let them go?"

"Am I sure?" He laughs without humor. "There's the question. No, I'm not sure, but it's what Alex wanted. I just haven't been able to bring myself to do it."

I wrap my arms around him, tilting my chin up to study him. "If I had anything that was my father's, I don't know if I could let it go, either."

"Have you visited any of his public displays?"

I shake my head. "I was afraid it would bring attention to me, so I didn't dare, and I also had to try to block out the past. It's how I got up every day."

"The blackouts tell me that came with a price."

"Isn't there always a price?"

"Sometimes there's happiness, Amy. And you deserve to experience that. I'm going to get you something of your father's."

"I just want the chance to say good-bye properly."

"We'll get you that, too."

In that moment, when I hear his desire to give me any connection to my family he can, I know that I'm devastatingly, completely in love with him. And though we haven't spoken the words, they sweep silently through the air, a current waiting to be charged.

I press to my toes and touch my lips to his, letting them linger a moment, and he sets his hand on my back, holding me to him, breathing with me. His presence in my life is like the lighthouse in stormy waters to a ship lost at sea.

Dragging my fingers over his goatee, I ease back and our eyes meet, triggering a mutual smile.

He leads me to another display case. "This is the only Egyptian display in the room. Four of them are replicas, unfortunately, but they're all antiques."

I'm immediately drawn to a dagger carved in ebony with copper trim, representing the mid-BCE. My hand flattens on the glass, flashes of a memory teasing my mind, transporting me back to a dig site. I'd been fourteen, on the last trip I'd ever take with my family.

"What is it?" I asked eagerly, tossing my braided hair over my shoulder as I dropped to the desert ground next to Chad, who was digging fiercely.

"I don't know. Some sort of limestone. Maybe a tool. Why aren't you at lunch with the others?"

"I finished early."

"Then make yourself useful. Go get help. Dad's going to want to see this."

I drop to my knees and start digging.

Chad grabs my arm and grimaces, dirt smudging his handsome, tanned face. "You know better. We need a team and proper equipment. Go get help."

"Father!" I shout at the top of my lungs.

"I said go get help, not shout for help. I could have done that myself."

"But you didn't, so it's a good thing you have me to think of the obvious, right?"

"A happy memory, for once?" Liam asks, snapping me back to the present.

I tilt my head. "What?"

"You're smiling."

"Oh. Yes. It was a happy memory." I give him a quick peck on the cheek.

"What's that for?"

"For helping me honor them with good memories."

The doorbell rings, and Liam says, "That'll be Tellar and Derek with lunch and the files for us to review."

"Lunch sounds wonderful," I say, linking my arm with his. "Rest has done wonders for my appetite."

I'm in good spirits as I sit down at the table with Liam, Tellar, and Derek, another memory without a blackout expanding my optimism for the prospects of recovering my past.

Eager to finish lunch quickly in order to learn about their research, I'm about to take a bite of my ham and cheese sandwich when splintering pain slices through my scalp.

I see the same dig site I'd been on with my brother. And I see him.

Oh, God. I see him.

TWELVE

HOT. IT'S SO VERY HOT. I lie in the tent, staring at the ceiling, thinking about how exciting the dig site had been today. My brother snorts out a loud snore that makes me laugh, and I turn my head to study him. He blinks awake, eyeing me through wayward locks of blond hair, and he grimaces. He often does that with me.

"Why aren't you asleep?" he grumbles.

"I'm excited. I want to know what you found today."

"We'll know tomorrow."

I roll to my side. "I wonder if we'll find more than that one piece of limestone?"

He drops his arm over his face. "Sleep, so we can get up early and find out."

"I have to pee." I open the tent, slip into the darkness, and glance at the starless sky, remembering how dark it was before the sandstorm we'd lived through last year. Terrifying doesn't begin to explain it. Quietly, I tiptoe past rows of tents; the silence is kind of creepy.

Finishing up at the portable bathroom, I hear the rumble of voices and follow the sound until I spot my father standing beside the supply tent. A covered truck that's not part of our normal caravan is parked next to it. Curious, I squat down and move through a row of tents to come up alongside one of the four Jeeps in the caravan, then peek around the side of the vehicle. Darn. The man my father's talking to has his back to me, but it's too dark to see anything anyway.

The man opens the truck door and the interior light illuminates the strained lines of my father's face. Discomfort burns in my belly and I'm instantly on edge, certain this meeting isn't a good one. The man hands my father a large envelope and my father glances inside.

"This isn't what we agreed on," my father says, his angry tone biting through the silence.

A breeze stirs the dry desert floor, swirling dirt into the air, and though I try not to, I begin to cough.

My father and the stranger turn to look at me . . .

"Amy. Amy! Damn it, Tellar, call Dr. Murphy," Liam commands.

"No," I gasp, discovering that I'm in Liam's lap. "I'm okay."

"Holy hell, woman, you scared the crap out of me. Again."

"Me too," Tellar agrees.

"Add me to the list," Derek chimes in. "I say call the doc."

"No," I insist. "I don't feel any pain. The memory wasn't bad. It was good."

He looks at me like I've finally lost it. "That was *not* good."

Tellar stands up and gives Derek a pointed look. "We should give them a few."

"No," I insist. "You both came here to help me get answers, and I've never needed them as much as I do right now." I try to get up but Liam holds me in place. I glower at him. "Let me sit back in a chair."

"You just—"

"Had a blackout. I get it. I've been having them for years."

"You weren't pregnant then."

The worry in his reply gives me pause, and I stroke his

cleanly shaven jaw. "Dr. Murphy knows about the flash-backs."

"She obviously doesn't know about you passing out and hitting your head in Denver, or she would have done more to stop them." His tone is pure disapproval. "I'm calling her today."

In my worry about ending this nightmare before the baby arrives, I didn't ask enough questions when I was with Dr. Murphy. I stroke my thumb over his neatly trimmed goatee. "She's meeting with us for an in-depth consultation on Monday. Let her have her weekend."

He scowls. "I'm not letting her send me out of the room this time."

"Agreed. Now can I go back to my chair?"

Looking less than pleased, he allows me to stand, but he isn't about to let go of me completely until I'm settled back at the table on my own. Tellar is still standing, and all three men stare at me like they expect me to black out again any second. And if it weren't for the baby, I'd almost wish they were right. I want to remember more, faster.

I flatten my palms on the sleek wood and begin revealing what I think is one of my most important flashbacks to date. "When I was in Egypt at one of the last dig sites I went to with my family, I saw the man from the black sedan, who . . . might have been having an affair with my mother in Texas." The admission is painful. "He was with my father."

Liam rolls his chair around to face me, and Tellar moves to sit back down. Apparently, I've gotten their attention.

"Who is he?" all three men ask at once.

"I don't have a name." I try to visualize the man's face, but can't. He'd turned around. I'd seen him. Hadn't I? "All I saw clearly was the back of his head and his profile—at least that's all I remember right now. It was the middle of the night, so it was dark, and all of the workers on the site were tucked away in tents and sleeping. I'd left mine to go to the bathroom. They were by a supply tent."

"Just your father and this man?" Derek asks.

"Yes, and . . ." I wet my suddenly parched lips. "I'm not sure why I hid, but I did. I tried to make out what was being said, but it was no different than the night this man was with my mother in Jasmine Heights. I couldn't hear much."

"Anything you heard could be helpful," Liam encourages, "even if you think it's not."

"The man handed my father an envelope. When my father looked inside, he was angry and raised his voice, and I heard him say that 'it,' whatever was in the envelope, wasn't what they'd agreed on."

I expect questions and comments, but all I get is blank looks that frazzle my nerves. "No," I reply to the accusations they don't speak.

Liam covers my hand, his expression as grim as his tone. "You know what it sounds like. You have to."

My defenses flare. "It wasn't some sort of payoff. We had investors and donations. It had to be that—or maybe it wasn't money at all. My point is simply that my mother was possibly having an affair with someone my father was doing business with." My throat tightens. "That somehow makes it worse."

Tellar interjects, "I started out working for a PI who specialized in cheating—" he seems to catch himself, "domestic disputes. It's common that the affair happens with someone close to the couple. I'd bet my two front teeth that this guy is at the root of all of this."

It was never about the money. I'd overheard my mother say that to someone. Who? And if someone claims it's not about the money, then money *is* involved.

Liam moves my sandwich closer to me. "Let's eat, and then we'll all dig into the files with that connection in mind."

I shake my head. "I don't want to eat. I want to look through the files now."

Liam sighs and motions to Derek. "Show her the pictures."

My brow furrows. "Pictures?"

Derek reaches down into the box he'd brought with him, retrieves a black three-ring binder, and sets it in front of me. "This holds every picture we could pull of anyone who ever crossed your path. Maybe you'll find your man in there."

I stare at the binder that holds the past I've tried to force into a dark corner, steeling myself for what I'll see. Yet when I flip it open, it's like a physical blow to see my mother staring back at me, her lovely blue eyes bright, her long blond hair like silk around her pretty face. But the blow is nothing compared to her screams for help echoing in my mind.

I squeeze my eyes shut, fighting the burning sensation that does nothing to help me or my mother.

Liam rolls his chair closer, his hand on my leg. "Tell me about her," he says softly.

I have to swallow twice before I whisper, "I can't. Not now." I swallow again. I think I might be sick.

"If you aren't up to this—"

"I am." I look at him, straightening my spine. "I have to be." I flip another page. Liam squeezes my leg and I cover his hand with mine, welcoming the strength he is to me.

Two hours later, I haven't found an image of the man, and I've looked at every photo twice.

Liam shuts the binder. "Clearly he's not in there—but a whole lot of pain is."

And he's right. I think I'll tell Dr. Murphy that I've diagnosed myself. It's not post-traumatic stress disorder. It's a broken heart.

"You have to eat, baby," Liam continues. "You haven't touched your sandwich."

"I might have something useful here," Derek interjects, typing something into his computer. "Being in real estate, I know that cities with Jasmine Heights's modest population of twenty thousand are booming, as it is, tend to have a primary investor who's making it happen. I looked into it, and I was right. Not only is one man the primary owner of most of the real estate, he's also a substantial investor in"—he pauses for effect— "the hospital that shows no record of you ever being there."

Of course it doesn't. To the world outside this room, I'm dead. "Who?" I ask and I don't sound urgent. The truth is, looking at those photos was like taking a knife and slicing me open. I'm bleeding inside and barely holding it together.

"His name is Sheridan Scott," Derek supplies. "Sound familiar?"

"No. But it might later, after I've had time to think."

Derek turns his computer to face Liam and me. "Do you recognize him?"

"No," I say, disappointment filling me as I stare at the image of a good-looking sixtysomething-year-old man in a suit, his dark hair peppered with gray. "He's way too old. My mother was in her forties. I'd guess the man I saw to have been her age or younger. Tall, and dark, and good-looking."

Liam moves his own computer in front of me and pulls up another photo for me to study.

I frown. "Why are you showing me Alex?"

"You've seen his photo?"

"I googled him back in Denver, when you told me about him."

His shoulders visibly relax. "I just wanted—"

"To build trust." I give the other men my back and cup his cheeks, not caring about the audience. "You have it." I press my lips to his, drinking in the connection to the one person in this world I *can* trust. And the thought eases the pain from the photos enough to make it bearable. He, like our child, gives me the light in the darkness to fight this battle. I have to keep fighting.

SATURDAY MORNING IS bittersweet. It begins with me in the shower with Liam, and we almost forget that the idea is to use soap and shampoo. Afterward, still craving that casual feeling of hanging around the house we'd had the day before, I convince Liam to dress in a navy Yankees sweatsuit I find in his drawer, and I choose a pale pink one of my own, minus the sports logo. We head to the kitchen to meet up with Tellar and Derek to do more research, but for a few more moments, I'm still all about Liam, the father of my child, and I'm amazed how, no matter what he wears, he owns the space around him. And yes, me too.

"The chef is in the house," Tellar announces when we arrive.

Liam and I join Derek at the table while Tellar moves around the kitchen like he owns it, and despite his cheery tone, his shoulder holster dents my mood.

Liam leans in and kisses me. "I need to make a couple of business calls." He eyes Tellar. "I expect the chef to still be in when I get back."

Tellar mock-salutes him. "At your command, sir."

Laughter bubbles from my lips and I murmur a greeting to Derek. For a moment, I have the oddest sense of being in a happy bubble that could burst at any moment, and I don't want it to.

Tellar sets a cup in front of me and fills it. "Decaf, per the boss's orders. And how about an omelet? Or eggs sunny side up? Name your egg."

"Scrambled eggs, well done, please." I lift the cup. "And thank you."

Derek and I chat for a few minutes about his sister, who's also a high-end real estate agent, and by the time I finish my eggs, Liam returns. Tellar whips him up an omelet and I listen as Derek and Liam talk about the Denver project Derek's still trying to salvage, which Liam was supposed to design.

Listening to them, I realize that the bond between them is far more brotherly than simple friendship. And I get why Derek is here. He and Tellar are the closest thing to family Liam has. Except for me and the baby.

I reach under the table and press my hand to Liam's leg. His hand covers mine and we exchange a warm gaze. Not for the first time, I'm moved by how alike we are. How alone we were in a world of billions of people, until we found each other. I know why he battles being over-protective. I can't bear to lose him or this child.

"Need anything else?" Tellar asks me.

I look at him curiously. "Why are you acting like a dot-ing papa bear?"

He shrugs. "You're pregnant, and my mom and four sisters taught me right."

"Four sisters?"

"That's right. Three of whom have had babies. So, I ask again. Need anything else?"

I glance at his gun, a tiny prick in my bubble. He's not just family. He's a trained protector and killer. "Yes," I reply. "I need you to not need the gun. I didn't notice it the first night we met."

"I use an ankle holster in public, but this is easier to access."

"Right. And you need it to be easy to access."

"This is where I tell her the truth," Tellar says to Liam, then turns to me. "Yes. I do."

"Yes, baby, he does," Liam agrees. "And I'd feel better if you had one, and knew how to shoot it."

"I don't like guns, but I can shoot. If I wasn't afraid the registration would make me more trackable, I'd have bought one long ago."

Liam leans back in his chair, his dark hair intensifying his aqua eyes. "Not the answer I expected."

"Yeah, well, it wasn't by choice, though I'm not beyond seeing the value of knowing how to protect myself. Learning to shoot was the condition for traveling with my father. He was concerned about females in a foreign country that isn't female-friendly."

Tellar sits down with a plate piled high with eggs, potatoes, and a bagel, and my eyes go wide. "Apparently lugging around a big weapon takes a lot of energy."

Tellar's eyes light up. "Don't you know it, honey."

Liam ignores the exchange, his elbows on the table, his focus on me. "Was your father's concern a general one, or based on a specific threat?"

"There were occasional issues over my mother and me not covering our faces and bodies."

Liam presses, "Anyone in specific you remember that we should look into?"

"No. No one specific. I can tell you think this is a potential lead, but really it's not that uncommon over there. It happens."

"An interesting thing about Sheridan Scott that's well-timed right now," Derek interjects. "He's not only richer than Liam, but he's richer because he's into oil. He's got a connection to Jasmine Heights, and now we've linked him to Egypt."

I twist in my seat to face him. "We weren't involved in oil," I say but even as I do I hear my mother shouting, and I hug myself against the shiver racing down my spine.

MONDAY MORNING COMES and Liam leaves me with Tellar to take care of business at the bank, but he's back in time for Dr. Murphy's visit.

"Why don't we just use the bed?" she suggests, very proper in a navy skirt suit, while I've opted for the distressed jeans and red sweater I want to wear before they no longer fit.

I sit on the edge of the mattress, and she joins me and begins checking my vitals. Liam, as promised, stays in the room.

"How is she?" Liam asks, towering over us, and looking incredibly male in a dark suit and pressed white shirt, his blue eyes glinting bluer with the sun and water behind him.

"Her vitals are good, and so was her blood work. I'm setting the due date as June twenty-sixth."

My eyes connect with Liam's and I expect excitement, but I find intensity, worry. He doesn't even comment on the date. "She hit her head a few months ago when she fell during a blackout, and she needed stitches."

"My recommendations haven't changed. Acupuncture and therapy. I can do an acupuncture session today before I leave." She glances at me. "Are you eating?"

I nod. "Yes. Now that I'm rested, I seem less nauseous."

"Can she travel?" Liam asks.

Dr. Murphy gives Liam a keen look. "Does she need to travel?"

"Yes."

"Where?"

"International. I'm not at liberty to tell you more."

"I need more, to prepare her vaccinations. She and the baby have to be protected."

"Go wide," Liam says. "We might start in one place and move to another."

"When are you leaving?"

"Tomorrow morning."

I'm on my feet in an instant, closing the short distance between him and me. *"Tomorrow?"*

His hands come down on my shoulders, warm and solid. "Yes. I told you to trust your instincts, and now I'm asking you to trust mine."

"I'll give you two a moment," Dr. Murphy says. "I need to call my office anyway."

Liam glances over my shoulder. "Any of the rooms on this floor are at your disposal."

She clears her throat. "If you want to give birth here, you need to be back by May first."

After I hear the door shut, I ask, "Where?"

"Taiwan. I have contacts there who can protect us, and I've already lined up medical care and a place for us to stay."

Taiwan. It's a long way from Texas. "What about paperwork?"

"I've arranged everything. We'll have what we need by morning. We need to do this."

This is the ultimate test, the confirmation that I trust him completely, and I reach deep, doing what I've always done to survive, and what Liam claims I've done well. I listen to my instincts, and they say I belong with this man.

I inhale and nod. "Yes. Okay."

THE TRUST I'VE given Liam seems to deepen our bond further, and with a touch, a look, he seems to anticipate every nervous moment I have. A moment no one else could have with me. Moments I'd never thought I'd share with anyone, ever.

Bedtime comes and I climb into bed. Liam brings my purse and sets it next to me. Then he lays a small leather case on the bed, unsnaps it, and shows me what's inside. "It's a Smith and Wesson thirty-eight. Compact and easy to fit in your purse." He presses it into my hand. "Comfortable?"

I close my eyes, swallowing the knot in my throat. "As comfortable as needing it is going to get." I check it, confirm it's loaded, and close it back into the case. "Thank you." I put it in the black Chanel purse and it fits perfectly.

Liam sets my bag on my nightstand, then climbs into bed with me. "I want to feel your skin," he murmurs, stripping away my gown and his boxers, and wrapping me in his strong arms, spooning me. This moment isn't about sex and passion. It's about hope, and fear, and the kind of loss neither of us want to feel again.

"Safety first," he reminds me, stroking my hair in that soothing way he does. "Answers second. I've got you, baby. I promise. I've got you, and I've got us."

My lashes lower, letting the scent of him, familiar and warm like his arms, ease the tension in my body. He's right. Safety first—but I can't escape this horrible feeling in my gut. Like once I leave, I'll never come back. Unable to fully sleep, I drift in and out of that thought. *Once I leave . . .*

Suffocating from the smoke pouring into my room, I shove open the window and suck in fresh air, but I'm not sure I want to breathe. My mother . . . she's stopped screaming. What does that mean?

"Mom? Mom, answer me!"

"Jump, Lara!" my brother shouts. "Jump now!"

"Not without you and Mom and Dad!" I shout back, angry at something, everything. Afraid of the orange flames licking a path through my door, ready to consume it as they had the hallway.

"You can see the flames, damn it!" he answers. "I can't get to you! I'm going out another window. I'll meet you outside."

The flames move closer and I perch on the edge of the window. He didn't say anything about Mom and Dad. "Is Mom okay? Did Dad get to her? Did he get her out?"

"Goddammit, Lara, how many times do I have to tell you to fucking jump! I'm running out of time. Get out, so I can get out!"

The flames jump to my bed and I scream. I barely remember perching on the windowsill, where I wobble and have to catch myself. It's dark and I can't see below, but I know the roof slants just below my window. Heat sears my back and I yelp, climbing out onto the roof and squatting, clinging to the window's ledge to keep from sliding into the darkness. Praying the fire trucks will come before I jump. Why aren't they coming? Why aren't they here?

Flames ignite the curtains and I let go of the window ledge, sliding down the roof on my stomach. "Please get them out, Chad! Please, all of you get out!"

My feet catch on the gutter, and it almost gives. Cautiously, I inch around and manage to squat. There's a tree near the roof, but it's so very dark, and I try to gauge how close the tree limb is. As I reach for the limb, a blast from inside shakes my bones and I'm thrown from the roof.

Gasping, I sit up, the sound of a screeching alarm tearing

through my ears. Fire alarm. Smoke bites viciously at my nose. *Oh, God. Oh, God. No.* I start to shake all over. *This can't be happening.*

Liam is standing over me, shouting something at me. I don't know what. I just know that the house is on fire. The house is on fire.

THIRTEEN

LIAM WRAPS AN ARM AROUND MY neck and pulls me to him, his mouth finding my ear while the alarm remains brutally loud. "Get dressed. And remember—I've got you, baby, and I've got us." Buck naked, he heads for the hallway.

He's got us. Heroic words that he believes, but so did my brother. So did my father. My heart lodged in my throat, I scramble off the bed, my adrenaline pumping, but I'm remarkably calm. I will not crumble. I will not be defeated. And I will not jump out the window alone again.

I tug on gray sweats and a T-shirt, and it's impossible to

escape the memory of doing the exact same thing six years ago. I'm just shoving my feet into tennis shoes when Liam appears, dressed in the Yankees sweatsuit.

"I smell smoke, but I see no fire." He has to practically shout to be heard over the alarm. "I called 911 and Tellar. It's an old house; it could be electrical."

I flinch; that's exactly what was said about my family home. He exits the closet and I follow, ready to get out of here. I know exactly how fast flames appear and consume a home. Liam grabs my purse and slides the strap of the crossbody over my head, and I know it's for the gun. He doesn't believe this is electrical or a coincidence, any more than I do. Our hunkering down inside had forced someone to act, either trying to kill us while we slept or, since there were no flames yet, to drive us out into the open.

Holding onto my hand, he enters the hallway and my stomach knots as we start down the stairs. I think of Alex's dagger collection we're leaving behind. Liam's piece of his past.

My teeth chatter with the intensity of the screaming alarms and a stunning realization washes over me. The alarms in my Texas home hadn't gone off. Not one—and we'd had several.

"Liam!" Tellar shouts. He appears on the bottom level staircase, and we follow him back down. "There's smoke at the lower right exterior of the house, but no flames," he reports over his shoulder.

As we reach the garage, I shiver at the November winter wind blasting in through the open doors.

He adds, "The gates to the house are open for the emergency crews, and Derek has security clearing the building next door, to be safe."

"Good. I don't want this exploding and leaping over there." Liam curses. "I have to go back for the travel documents."

Anxiety shoots through me. "What? *No*. That's insanity. You can't go back inside the house. You *can't*."

He cups my face. "I'm getting you out of here *before* I can't." He eyes Tellar, his jaw as steely as his tone. "Do *not* let her out of your sight." He lifts me by the arms and pretty much hands me to Tellar.

"No, Liam!" I jerk forward but Tellar shackles my waist. "Don't do this, Liam! Don't go in the house again!" But he's already running back toward the door.

"What's happening? Where's Liam?"

At the sound of Derek's voice, I seize the distraction and kick Tellar.

He grunts. "Damn it. Stop it, Amy."

"He's in the house, Derek!" I squirm against Tellar, trying to see Derek. "Do you hear me? He's in the *house*. You're not on his payroll. You don't have to listen to Liam and let him get himself killed."

"That's low, Amy," Tellar snaps, then says to Derek, "Liam's fine. He went back in to grab some paperwork."

"He's *not* fine," I insist, twisting in his arms. Finally I manage to free myself enough to face him. "Let me go, Tellar!"

"There are no flames, Amy. He's fine, and I'm not letting you run back into the house."

"If there are no flames and he's fine, why can't I go in?" I challenge.

A fire truck roars loudly into the driveway—and pain splinters through my head. I lean into Tellar, pressing my face into his shirt, and for a moment I'm back on the roof of my house, reaching for that tree limb and being blasted off the edge.

Tellar starts dragging me out of the garage, snapping me back to the present. I'd assumed the blast at my house had been from the fire, but . . . I dig in my heels and yank hard on his arm. "I think there was a bomb in my house in Texas. What if there's one now? Get him out of the house! Get Liam out *now*!"

"Fuck," Tellar growls and shoves me at Derek. "Get her away from the house."

As Tellar runs toward the house my vows to stay calm

evaporate, leaving me with nothing but panic. My mother's screams play in my head, shredding my mind and soul. I hear Chad yelling for me to jump. I should have stayed to help him, but he died—and now Liam is going to die. Everyone I love dies. And God, what if Tellar dies now, too?

I start fighting Derek to get to Liam and Tellar. I screwed up. I did this all wrong. A sob rips from my throat, and sounds are coming from me that I don't recognize.

Derek curses. "You're going to hurt yourself, and I can't let that happen." He bends at the waist and hikes me over his shoulder, and I yelp with the insanity of the moment as he starts to run.

Blood rushes to my face, tears pouring over my forehead, and I suck in so much cold air that I start to cough.

Firemen are everywhere. People are everywhere. I can't breathe or think, until finally, Derek slides me to my feet.

The minute I see the concern in his eyes, I sob and melt against him. "I can't lose him. I can't."

He holds me to him, hugging me. "You're not going to lose him. I promise."

I push back and glare at him. "Like my brother promised he was coming out of the house? Like that, Derek?"

"Amy—"

"Because he didn't come out." My voice is ripped with heartache. "He. Didn't. Come. Out. None of them came out."

Suddenly I'm pulled around, and Liam wraps me in his strong arms. Relief washes over me and I can finally breathe again. "Oh, thank God."

The warmth of his palms frames my face. "I'm okay. We're okay."

"It's not okay. It's not. I told you to stop saying that. Just because you say it does not make it so, Liam. You think it does. You think you can will it, whatever 'it' is, at the moment to happen, and make it so. You think—" He scoops me up and starts walking. "Stop picking me up. Stop acting macho before it gets you killed."

"She's pregnant," he tells a fireman. "I need her checked out."

"I don't need—" I begin.

"You do," Liam insists, walking toward an EMS truck and a man in uniform. "She needs to be checked, but give us a minute, will you?" he says.

The man moves aside and Liam climbs into the truck, setting me on the bed inside and joining me.

I slide my hand to his leg. "You shouldn't have gone back in. You shouldn't—"

He leans in and kisses me, the touch of his mouth on mine sending warmth through me. "Don't ever do that to me again," I whisper. "It was like having my heart ripped from my chest."

"I wouldn't scare you or hurt you on purpose." He curls my hand in his. "Talk to me about the bomb."

"I remember being on the roof of my house. I was trying to get to the tree to jump, and the house exploded."

"Fire can do that, baby."

"But the alarms in the house didn't go off. Not one of them, Liam."

His expression darkens. "Listen to me, Amy. They've brought in bomb-sniffing dogs, and that brings questions and complications. Don't talk about this to anyone. Tell them you were panicked and hysterical."

I nod. "I don't believe this was a coincidence. So if there wasn't a bomb or a fire, why do this?"

"Good question, and exactly why we need to leave the country."

"Excuse me, Mr. Stone." Liam twists around to glance at the police officer standing at the end of the EMS vehicle, who says, "Can I ask you both some questions?"

"Me, yes," Liam replies. "Not her. She's pregnant. I don't want her stressed." Liam doesn't give the officer a chance to object, turning back to me. "I'll be right outside. I'm sending the EMS guy in to check you out." He presses his cheek to mine. "We're out of here the instant we navigate the red tape—sooner, if I get worried."

Once he leaves, a fortysomething EMS worker climbs inside with me. "How are you feeling?"

"I'm fine now." The uncertain look he gives me tells me he probably saw my meltdown. "Really. I'm fine."

He squats in front of me. "Let's get your vitals, to be sure."

The rumble of Liam's voice tells me he is near, and the fact that I really don't want to answer questions keeps me on the bed. "Yes, please."

A few minutes later, he finishes up. "You're all clear, but I think you should rest here until we can get you to the hospital to check out the baby."

"The baby?"

"Is fine," he says. "But it's always good to be careful. Safety first."

"Right," I say of the words Liam had used before we'd gone to sleep and for some reason I think of the gun in my purse. "Safety first."

A fireman appears at the end of the truck and motions to the man, who excuses himself and goes to speak with him. I can still hear Liam, but it's impossible to make out anything he's saying.

The EMS worker returns and squats beside me again. "Special delivery. You have someone worried about you who can't get past security." He hands me a folded note. "From your brother, I'm told."

My heart begins to thunder in my ears and everything around me seems to tilt. Chad is alive? It can't be. But . . . I'm alive. Even though I'm officially dead.

The EMS tech pats my leg. "I need to call in to my boss on the radio. If you want to get a message to your brother, let me know." He moves to the front seat of the vehicle.

I stare at the piece of paper, my heart in my throat. I'm afraid to open it and have my sudden hope shattered, but I have to know. I flip it open and read the unfamiliar writing.

Amy,

I wish I could say this in person. This is Meg. I know you think I work at the Denver real estate office, but I'm actually your sister-in-law. Chad didn't die in the fire. He hid, like he hid you. They found him right after he moved you to Denver. Now they want something from us, or they're going to kill him. They think you and I both know what that is. I hope you do, because I don't. We have to save Chad.

I'm not sure what's up with Liam. I think he could be involved, or after whatever they're after. If he's not and he gets in the middle of this, they'll kill him, like they do anyone who gets in their way.

I'm in a cab across the street. I'm sure you know, but cell phones are traceable. Leave yours. Just walk out of the open gate and come to me. No one is expecting that. Hurry, before you can't. Chad's life depends on it.

Bile rises in my throat, the acid burn of emotions that shift and change from second to second, almost too much to handle.

Chad is alive? Meg is his wife? Liam is involved?

I expect to feel joy over Chad and heartache over Liam . . . but in my heart, I believe nothing in this letter. This is a trap. The moment there was a threat to Liam, I was snagged.

Aware that Liam's just outside the ambulance and could

return at any moment, I have limited time to think through all the ways every next step I take could go wrong. I open my purse and dig for a pen, my gaze landing on the leather case and the weapon nestled in its depths. And I silently thank Liam for the protection it offers. It also tells me he is protecting me. He's *not* a part of the hell I'm running from.

Shutting my purse, I decide to leave Liam the note from Meg, so he knows exactly what's happening. I know he'll come after me, and he needs a way to find me. If only I had a phone. I start to write.

Liam—

I don't know if Chad is alive. I only know that there's a clear threat to your life in this note. I'm leaving the note so you see you are in danger. I know you'll look for me, but don't get killed doing it. Losing you would destroy me.

I hesitate only a moment, reminding myself life is too short for regrets, and I add,

I love you.
Amy

I fold the note, write Liam's name in big bold letters, and with great regret, drop it on the stretcher. Inching to the edge of the truck, a ball of pressure forms in my chest when

I see Liam to the right, his back to me. Nothing would please me more than to run up and hug him, and I vow that moment will come sooner, not later. I eye the two police officers who are talking to him, and consider cutting to my left and out of sight around the edge of the truck. But without a view of what awaits, I risk running into Tellar or Derek.

My gaze settles on some sort of mini–fire truck with hoses directly ahead of me and I decide it's my best cover. Liam's broad shoulders and wide stance offer adequate cover from the cops, and I draw a breath and just go for it. Calmly, careful not to bring attention to myself, I climb out of the truck and start walking. And I keep walking, moving past the mini-truck and straight toward the exit, where the gates remain open, with nothing but orange traffic cones as a deterrent to those coming and going.

I'm on the street with not so much as a question asked of me, and I scan for the cab, finding it to the left of the gate. I glance over my shoulder, some part of me hoping Liam will come charging after me, while another is relieved he is not. More regret burrows deep in my gut, but I know I have to do this.

Darting across the street, I slip my hand in my purse, unsnap the case around the gun, and slip it free. My hand is on the handle when I stop at the cab and yank open the door, giving myself a split second to register that it's really Meg inside.

"Amy." She breathes my name like it's relief, when it feels dangerous on her tongue, wrong.

"Hurry," she urges. "Before you're seen."

I don't move. I can't seem to make myself get in the car.

She shoves a photo at me and I stare at it, then gasp at the image I haven't been able to fully form in my mind of my brother's face staring back at me, his arm is wrapped around Meg's shoulder. He's with her.

"He's . . . he's alive." I can't breathe, all over again.

"Not for long, if we don't do something. Help me save him, Amy. Please. I beg you. Help me save him."

Chad is alive. Chad is alive! I get into the cab and pull the door shut.

FOURTEEN

"GO!" MEG SHOUTS AT THE DRIVER, and I remember the moment at the Denver airport with Liam chasing after me. When I'd been running from the wrong thing and the wrong person.

The cab pulls away from the curb and Meg throws her arms around me. "Thank God you're okay."

Reluctantly, I return the hug that seems meant more for family than virtual strangers, unable to fight my unease. Shifting away from her, I take the photo she holds, staring at the image, thankful for the streetlights that allow me to soak in the way Chad's blue eyes are lit up with a smile, and how his longish blond hair curls just a bit at his forehead and brows.

My gaze lifts to Meg's, her pale blond hair a shade not unlike my brother's, and I see no discomfort at my intense inspection, just more sympathy—though I'm not sure for what. Pain, maybe? Fear? Confusion? Do they radiate off of me, the way control and confidence do off of Liam?

Her hand covers mine where I'm holding the photo, and I don't miss the obvious symbolism of the choice. "I have more pictures of him. He's alive, Amy," she vows. "We have to keep him that way."

My lips part and there is a burn at the back of my throat and in my belly. I'm not ready to believe yet and risk the heartache of loss all over again. "Tell me everything. I need to know everything."

She glances at the driver and back at me. "When we're alone. I don't trust anyone. I just don't."

I sink back on the seat and clasp the picture to my chest. *Don't trust anyone.* The same lesson my handler— my brother?—had given me quite effectively without any real conversations, but then, actions speak louder than words.

Meg sinks down next to me, too close, I think. She laughs without humor. "Ironic, right?"

My brows dip. "What?"

"I just told you I don't trust anyone, and now I want you to trust me."

Ironic. Yes. Very. "I just want Chad back."

"Then we want the same thing."

No. If that were true, Liam would be here. "I have questions. Lots of questions."

"As you should."

"Why didn't you tell me who you were before now?"

"Not now," she cautions. "When we're alone and safe. We need to focus on safety and the speed of our departure. A man like the one you just left behind will shut down this city to stop you, if he can."

I get her discretion, but I don't like how she's avoided his name. "What do you mean, a man like him?"

"Rich and obsessed. It's a dangerous combination."

My defenses prickle. "He's far more than you give him credit for."

"Oh, I give him plenty of credit—which is exactly why I told our driver to take us across the Brooklyn Bridge. We need out of this city before he can stop us."

I stare out of the window, repeating her words in my head. Out of this city. I would have said the exact same thing forty-eight hours ago, and I guess that should be comforting. She's thinking like I was thinking. Even Liam wanted to leave sooner—but together. We were supposed to be together.

Thirty minutes later, I've spent the drive replaying conversations I've had with Meg in the past, looking for warning signs, but there isn't much to go on. We exit the cab at a chilly subway station, and I eye Meg's jeans, black knee-high boots and black leather jacket with envy. "Where to now?" I ask, hugging myself and not looking forward to being braless in a subway, especially at whatever time it is. I don't even know.

"I left my car in Albany."

"How far is that?"

"Three hours, with one stop to change trains. *If* we can catch the last train out at twelve-thirty. Otherwise we have to find a cheap hotel and hole up, which gives anyone looking for us time to organize." She eyes her dainty silver watch. "We're cutting it close. We'd better run."

We head down the subway stairs and unbidden, Liam's voice plays in my head: run *to* me, Amy, not from me. I'm trying, I think. I really am trying, and I hate the hell I must be putting him through.

An hour later, Meg and I have completed the trip to the train station and have boarded the train to Albany, settling uncomfortably into the hard plastic seats, with cool air blasting me from above. With no one near us for several rows front and back, we're in the perfect place to talk without anyone eavesdropping.

I lean against the window and face her. "Tell me about Chad. Tell me everything."

"He's everything to me, and I'll do whatever it takes to get him back."

She says the words with conviction and emotion, so why am I struggling to believe her? "How did you meet him?"

"I was a full-time student, working at a diner to pay the bills, when he started coming in during my shifts. We flirted quite a bit. Still, he never asked me out. I wasn't sure what to think. Then one night this creepy customer was drunk and he tried to . . . he was inappropriate. Chad punched him and I was rattled. Really rattled. It reminded me . . ." She cuts her gaze away a moment and draws a breath.

"I had some bad stuff with my stepfather, and I left the diner in the middle of my shift. Chad came after me, clearly worried. No one had worried about me for a very long time, but he hadn't ever asked me out and I was afraid he just felt sorry for me. Like he had some kind of hero complex about saving damsels in distress. But I found out later he was worried about his job and my safety."

My brows dip. "His job? What was his job?"

"He told me he did high-profile consulting that required complete anonymity and confidentiality."

"Meaning what?"

"I don't know."

I now sympathize with how Tellar felt when I said the same thing to him. "You mean you married him, and never knew what he did for a living?"

"I just thought it was a government security thing, or something to that effect. New York has plenty of—"

"New York. Are you telling me my brother lived in New York?"

"Yes. A few blocks from you. He told me you were in a witness protection program."

Witness protection? Was I? Could that be true? "Did he go by Chad?"

She shakes her head. "David Chad Wilson. He told me he preferred Chad, but his legal name was David. I didn't know any differently until the night we moved you to Denver."

"What happened that night?"

"He told me he was the reason you were in hiding, and . . . he told me about the fire."

"Did he tell you who set it?"

"No names. He said his work had put him in the crosshairs of some very rich, very powerful men, who thought he had something they wanted. I didn't ask him a lot of questions. It was simply part of being with him, and at the time of his confessions he was in crisis mode trying to move you

and us before it was too late. I figured I'd ask for more details when we were safe."

"So he felt you were both in harm's way, too?"

"Oh yes. And it was destroying him to think he'd put me
in danger by marrying me. Not that we were really married.
He'd used an alias."

Her voice cracks, and guilt twists in me over how I've
doubted her. "He had to. You know he had to."

"Yes. I just wish he'd told me. I love him. I'd do anything
for him. I'd die for him, Amy."

I think of Liam's words. *Anyone who wants to hurt you
has to come through me first.* He'd die for me, and I can't let
that happen. "No one else is going to die. I . . . my parents . . ."

"No." Her voice is soft, reluctant. "They didn't make it,
honey. Chad had nightmares over their loss, and he'd wake
up screaming. And I don't know what happened, but he
went nuts when he needed to move you to Denver. He was
terrified of losing you, too."

My gut clenches. Did I cause all of this by taking the job
at the museum?

"I helped him get the note to you in the museum and
set you up in Denver," she continues. "We were going to do
the same thing as before and live near you, but we weren't
there long before he said he had to take a trip. He was sup-

posed to be back in a day, but he never returned. He just vanished. I didn't know what to do. He'd set up certain things to help you, and I only knew some pieces of the puzzle. And he'd left me money, but I knew it wouldn't last forever. I was trying to maintain your cover, but I didn't fully understand." She shakes her head. "I tried, Amy. I did, but I was scared and—"

I grab her hand, grateful for her help. "It's okay. You did fine." But nothing is making any more sense now than it has for six years, and I feel like I've lost Chad in the same instant I've found him. "Are you sure Chad was kidnapped?"

"Yes. Absolutely. When you disappeared, I was confused. I started to think maybe he'd simply left me. That was easier to deal with than thinking he was dead. I didn't have a lot of money, but I went back to New York. It was the only link I had to you and Chad. I knew you'd been with Liam, so I took a job in the building next to his home, and got to be friends with a waitress at one of the restaurants he frequented. People buzzed about him when he was in town, but he wasn't there. You weren't there. Looking back, I think taking that job was a mistake. Either they already knew who I was and were watching me, or they were watching Liam for you, and found me because I was there. I don't know. Something went wrong, or right. Maybe it's good, because now we know he's alive."

"You haven't told me how we know he's alive."

She reaches into her purse and pulls out a five-by-eight-inch sealed envelope. My heart starts to race and acid burns my throat as I take it and lift the seal. Inside is a note and a small cell phone. I pull out the plain white notecard and open it.

WE HAVE CHAD. YOU HAVE WHAT WE WANT. GET IT FOR US OR HE DIES. YOU HAVE FIVE DAYS. DON'T MAKE US KILL HIM. WE'LL BE IN TOUCH.

The world is spinning, spinning, spinning, and I can't think. Adrenaline spikes in my blood. I can't catch my breath.

"I don't know what they want," Meg says. "I had to get to you, and I heard Liam was back in his house. I thought you could be there, and that you might know and—"

My gaze rockets to her. "You set Liam's house on fire to get to me?"

"I read about how to cause electrical fires that would be slow, and—"

"So you did it."

"I had no option. I had to get you out if you were inside. You *have* to see that. You have to want to save Chad the way I do. *Please* understand. Please. I'm sorry." Her bottom lip quivers and trembling tears drip from her eyes. "I'm alone, too. He's all I have. I have to save him."

I start to shake all over, and it's like her tears are my tears, and they streak my cheeks. "He's alive?"

"I hope so. I think so. He has to be."

"He's alive," I repeat, and suddenly we're hugging each other, both sobbing uncontrollably.

"Yes. He's alive. I hope he's alive. We have to keep him that way."

"We will," I vow. "We will." Memories of Chad flood my mind and I find myself rejoicing in his life, and mourning my parents all over again.

How long we hold each other, two aching hearts trying to survive, I don't know. But the vow to keep Chad alive burns inside me with as much heat as the fire that almost stole him away six years ago.

"We have to call Liam," I say, pulling back and wiping my eyes. "He can help. He has the resources to find Chad."

"No. That's why I had to get you out of there the way I did. I know you trust him, but Chad didn't, Amy. He was freaking out about Liam. He's got to be a part of this."

"No. That makes no sense. He's protected me."

"Why? To gain your trust? To get answers? Think about it, Amy. How did you end up in first class going to Denver? And why was a billionaire on a commercial flight?"

I laugh. "You don't know Liam Stone." I think of the single car in his garage. "He came from nothing, and he skimps in areas other people wouldn't." And while I haven't figured out fully why that is, it is, and that's my answer.

"How did you get into first class?"

"I don't know. Maybe Liam paid to get me there."

"Exactly. Don't you get it? Chad said he was trouble, and that we had to get him away from you." She grabs my arms and her voice quakes as she insists, "Liam Stone is the enemy."

FIFTEEN

MEG'S WORDS HANG IN THE AIR and she stares at me expectantly. I'm not sure what she expects me to say or do, but I have a fleeting memory of the moment Liam had ripped the center of my dress with the dagger, and I can almost feel the gentleness of his touch and kiss when we'd finally landed on the mattress. To me, Liam Stone is a man of infinite possibilities, but all of them add up to one simple fact: He's the man I love.

"We have to do this on our own," Meg insists when I

apparently don't speak up soon enough. "We can't trust anyone."

"We don't even know what they want—unless there's something you haven't told me."

"You're his sister. You have to know. Why else would he hide you like he did?"

Is she serious? "I'm his sister who was barely eighteen when she listened to her family being burned alive. I was sent into hiding with no explanations, and believing him dead."

She shakes her head, rejecting . . . what? My claim? The events? "You have to know what they want," she insists.

"I don't. Who was the man who met me outside the hospital? Surely he knows."

"What man?"

Right. She met Chad years later. "Did you meet any of Chad's friends?"

"He had no friends. I think that's why we needed each other. He was alone. I was alone."

My heart twists with how much her words remind me of me and Liam. "Then it looks like we're starting from scratch, and that isn't good. I've spent six years trying to put together a puzzle without pieces. Now we have five *days*."

"Four days. Now we have four. What are we going to do? We have to figure it out." Her voice rises, and she's starting to sound hysterical. "They think *I* know what they want, but I don't. I thought you'd know. What do we do, Amy?"

Call Liam. But she's so far off the deep end I don't dare press her on that. I grab her arms, leveling her in a stare. "We'll be okay." I nearly cringe at hearing myself utter the words I've forbidden Liam from saying to me. "We'll figure it out."

She inhales and lets it out on a choppy nod. The uniformed conductor passes and I release her to stop him, eager for a blanket. "Fifteen dollars for a blanket and pillow," he informs me.

I feel myself pale, and my bravado of seconds before fades. I have no money, no phone, no resources.

"I've got it," Meg offers quickly, and pays for a pillow and blanket for each of us.

Unwrapping mine, I snuggle beneath it, and remind myself that one phone call to Liam will change my situation. I'm choosing to give away control, and that *is* control, as he'd say. My confidence returns. "What's the plan once we get to your car?"

"We don't have one."

Wonderful. Terrific. "Do you have money? Can we get a cheap motel?"

"Yes. I have enough."

"Albany's a logical place to get off the train, from what I

could tell from looking at the destinations in the station. And I've learned the hard way that logical choices are dangerous. After we pick up your car there, we should head to a large metropolitan city and stop to rest there."

"Yes. Okay."

Now she has the "okay" disease. It's almost as bad as the "do nothing" disease I've lived with for six years. I sink back into the seat. "So what's the closest big city?"

"Philadelphia, maybe." She frowns. "It's kind of backtracking, so that might be smart. But really, why hide out? They've found us already, and they have Chad."

"What happens when they decide that they don't need us, but we know too much?" I ask.

"Right. Big city it is." She takes out her phone and checks the internet. "Philly is less than four hours."

"Philly it is, then," I agree. I settle my pillow under my head. "We should try to sleep. It's a long drive on no rest."

She hugs me. "I'm so glad you're here." Inching backward, she tilts her head and runs her hand through my long blond hair. "You're beautiful, like he was."

Discomfort ticks down my spine and I manage an awkward, "Thank you. We should rest."

She nods and sinks down in her seat.

I roll to my side, giving her my back, and I can't shake her choice of words. Beautiful like he *was*.

WHEN WE EXIT the train station, we head to Meg's expensive, grass-green Volvo. "Chad bought it for me," she says, reading the question in my eyes.

"Nice choice," I murmur. But as I settle into the leather seat, thankful for the seat warmers, the car bothers me. I was barely surviving most of the time, and Chad paid cash for her Volvo, and paid to garage it in Manhattan? It doesn't feel right—but then, he couldn't just hand me money. It would have brought attention to both of us.

With my driving turn coming up, I can feel the heaviness of exhaustion in my body, and I close my eyes, willing myself to rest, since I hadn't on the train. I have to consider my health, and I need a clear mind to decide what to do next. Four days is all I have left to discover what's been a six-year mystery. And even if I do, it won't be as simple as figuring out what these people want. It's figuring out how we get these people what they want, and how not to get killed in the process. And I wonder why, in Meg's panic, she hasn't thought of this.

I bring an image of Chad to my mind, and a smile curls my lips. *Chad . . .*

I wave good-bye to my best friend, Dana, as she pulls her Volkswagen out of the drive, and I run up the porch stairs, my eyes going wide at the sight of Chad sitting on one of the chairs.

"Chad!" I rush to him, and he's on his feet at the same instant I fling myself around him. "I can't believe you're here!" He's been away forever, first at college and then in Egypt. "Is Dad with you?"

"Yeah, but you know, he and Mom have to catch up." He waggles a brow. "At least they have a door. Those tent sessions they used to have could get awkward."

I laugh and we settle into the seats. He kisses my head. "How's school?"

"Miserable," I confess. "I want to be in the field with you and Dad. So does Mom."

"Finish school. It's good for you."

"You left college," I point out.

"Dad needed me in the field—and I didn't leave. I'm working for school credit, and there are windows of time when I'm in class."

"Right. I guess."

He sighs. "How's Luke?"

"He took off for college in Austin."

"Good thing I'm not there much. I don't like the way the bastard looks at you. He's lucky I don't beat his ass."

I've missed how he protects me. I miss our family. "Why do you hate him so much?"

"He's a user, known for bed-hopping and then bragging af-
terwards. I don't want you becoming a conquest."

"Like you don't bed-hop."

"Out of necessity and because I'm not a one woman kind of
man. I don't live a life that can support a girlfriend, but I don't
brag, and I don't make promises I can't keep."

Because he's a good-bye waiting to happen. "When do you
leave again?"

"Two days."

An ache forms in my chest. Two days. "Oh."

"We'll be back for your eighteenth birthday."

In six months? I guess I'm supposed to cheer up now.

A loud sound jolts me, and I sit up. "What happened?"

"We need gas," Meg announces, and I glance around to
find we're at a gas station and her door is open. "You've been
asleep about an hour."

"Asleep," I repeat, and frown at Luke's name in my head.
I know why I dreamed of my brother, but why does Luke
keep showing up in my dreams? But at least they *are*
dreams, not flashbacks with blackouts.

"Want anything from inside?" Meg asks.

My stomach rumbles. "I need a snack, but I think I'll go
to the bathroom."

"Just get whatever you want and put it at the register."
She climbs out of the car and shuts the door.

Grabbing my purse, I go still with a memory. My fake boss in Denver was named Luke. *I don't like the way the bastard looks at you. He's lucky I don't beat his ass.* My fist balls over my racing heart. Bossy, macho Chad had been trying to tell me he wanted to beat Liam's ass.

"Damn it," I whisper. "He's not the enemy."

Shoving open the car door and shivering against the cold, I glance at Meg over the hood. "I'm freezing. I need clothes and a coat to make it the next few days."

"Oh, gosh, yes. I'm sorry." She pops the trunk and opens it, revealing a couple of suitcases. She unzips one and hands me a jacket with a hood. "We can grab you some stuff on the road, too."

I nod and slip on the jacket. "Any idea why Chad would have put a camera in the computer you gave me in Denver?"

She snorts and shuts the trunk. "Yeah. He didn't trust Liam Stone. He was determined to find a connection between him and the men Chad was in trouble with."

I was right; the name Luke had been no accident. But it's just creepy, thinking my brother would tape me. What if he'd seen Liam and I having sex? The thought is gagworthy.

I refocus on Meg. "Did he find a connection to Liam?"

"No. Not before he . . . you know. I'm shocked you found out about the camera. He was sure you wouldn't."

I don't say anything. I'm confused by how she keeps claiming not to know anything about how Chad had set up my living situation, and yet she knows so much. My gaze goes to the store, and it hits me that I can call Liam and tell him I'm okay. I need to hear his voice. I know he needs to hear mine.

As I start walking, Meg calls out, "Amy." Turning, I tilt my head in a silent question, and she says, "Either he's one of them, and he'll kill us the minute he has what he wants, or he's not, and they'll kill him for getting involved."

Suddenly the ice in my blood is far colder than the winter air chilling my bones. I don't reply. She's right. I can't involve him. I have to let that idea go. I give her a choppy nod and start walking, and it hits me that I was wrong. She *has* thought about what happens when and if we hand over whatever these people want from us.

Inside the store I find the bathroom, where I lock the door and let air rush out of my lungs. *Think, Amy. Think.* But nothing comes to me. I have no plan. I walk to the sink and the girl in the mirror is a horror show of puffy eyes, no makeup, and witchy blond hair. My hand rests on my belly, where my reason above all else to survive rests. I'm going to figure out an answer. I just have no idea how.

Wanting the comfort the gun offers, I flip open my purse, and instead stare at the contents: a makeup bag that I unzip to find well stocked, a brush, hairspray, and a wallet. If the makeup bag is stocked . . . I grab the wallet and flip it open to stare at the wad of cash inside and the American Express black card. Liam has made sure I'm taken care of, and then some.

Without a bra to tuck the cash into, I take off my shoes and distribute it between them. Then I hold the credit card in my hand, certain it's being monitored. One swipe at a register would tell him where I am, and Meg's warning rolls through my head. *They'll kill him.* It's not the first time she's said it. I'm convinced that at least that part of her story is true. And Chad being alive—I believe that, too. One swipe of the credit card and I know Liam will be alerted to where I am. I stick the credit card in my shoe as a dire emergency plan, and my way to reach Liam when I'm ready. Which will be when I know he won't end up dead.

Meg is at the register when I exit, and I gather a couple of protein bars and some fruit. We're just settling into the car when Meg's phone rings. Her eyes go wide, terror in their depths. "My purse." She starts scrambling for it. "Where is it? That's the phone. That's the one they gave me."

My heart jackhammers and I search behind us and on the floorboard, finding the purse and handing it to Meg. The phone stops ringing before she can get it.

"No!" She hits the steering wheel, her head dropping onto it, her long hair draped over her face.

"Try to call it back," I urge, wondering why I doubt someone this distraught, but I do.

She lifts her head, tears streaking her cheeks. "Been there, done that. It doesn't work."

The phone beeps with a text, and she glances down and goes even paler.

"What is it?" I whisper, barely able to breathe.

She hands me the phone and I read the message, my blood running cold.

You're wasting time that Chad doesn't have in gas stations and on highways. Get on a damned plane and get me what I want, or your lover boy is dead.

Meg grabs my arm, her fingers pinching into my flesh. "What do we do? What the hell do we *do*?"

There's only one answer, and it's both right and wrong in every way: We go to Texas, where this started, and where deep down, I've always known it will end.

Liam will look for me there, and it's clear we're being watched, but I've warned him he's in danger. He'll be cautious and watch me from a distance—like they, whoever they are, seem to be doing.

I might even be safer for that reason. He won't charge into Jasmine Heights and claim me as his. Who am I kidding? This is Liam Stone I'm talking about. Yes. Yes, he will. And these people I'm dealing with have killed before, and they'll kill him if I don't find a way to protect him.

Meg grabs my arm. "Amy. Please. What do we do?"

"We go to a cheap hotel, where we shower, change, eat real food, and sleep for at least two hours. Then we figure it out."

"We should figure it out now!"

"No, we need to figure it out *right*. If we make the wrong move, people die." And that, I won't accept.

SIXTEEN

THREE HOURS LATER, WE'RE BACK ON the road and pulling into the airport. I've borrowed a bra that's a size too big, a pink tank top, jeans, and a jacket from Meg, and I feel at least a little human.

Meg parks her Volvo in the long-term lot at the Philadelphia airport, and hangs up the phone after calling the airline. "We're good. The flight that leaves in thirty minutes is still underbooked."

"How underbooked?"

"Thirty percent."

"Perfect. We can buy a ticket at the gate right now and get a seat."

"Liam Stone has money and power. He'll be able to see that you used your ID for the flight, and that's why I have to distract him. I assume that phone you're using is under an alias, since you helped Chad relocate me?"

She nods. "Yes."

"Then I'll use it to call Liam."

Her eyes go wide. "What? Are you crazy?"

"I'm going to convince him I'm in Denver and on the run. He'll get everyone who's working for him focused on finding me there. It won't keep him away forever, but it might be long enough for me to figure this all out." She doesn't look overjoyed. *I'm* sure not. "It's the best solution we have."

She hands me the phone. "You have to make him believe you're in danger."

I take it and turn away. "I know." And I dread doing that, clear to my soul. I take a moment to think up my story, then punch in his number.

He answers immediately, and how he knows it's me, I don't know, but he says, "Amy?"

The dark, gravelly richness of his voice runs down my spine and I can barely breathe.

"Amy? Is that you, baby? I need to hear your voice. Tell me it's you."

The desperation and worry in his voice rips through me like a blade. "I can't talk," I whisper. "I snuck a phone. I'm in Denver. I . . . oh, God. They're coming. I . . . Denver, Liam. I don't know where, and—" I hang up and drop my head, willing myself not to cry. A horrible knotting sensation starts in my stomach, and I pop the door open and vomit.

"Amy. Oh, God. Amy, are you okay?" Meg shoves a paper napkin at me.

I take it, wipe my mouth, and grab the borrowed navy jacket and my purse. "Let's go before we miss this flight."

INSIDE THE AIRPORT, Meg and I head to the bathroom, but the minute she's in the stall, I dart away and find a locker to store my gun. It kills me to leave it behind, but I can't take it on the plane. She's frantic when she finds me, of course, but I soothe her by telling her I was looking for a ginger ale for my stomach.

Now I'm unarmed, and on a plane headed toward certain danger. I spend the first hour of the flight dozing off and on with Liam's voice in my head. *Is that you, baby? I need to hear your voice.* I love him. I love the way he calls me *baby*. I love that he cares so much, and I hate what I did to him on that call. I hate it so much.

Somehow I force down the snack that's served, and sleep afterward. I wake to my hand hitting a stack of pictures Meg has set on my lap. I can barely swallow as I look at shots of Chad. There's one of him laughing, and there are fine lines by his eyes that didn't used to be there. This is a recent shot, the six years showing in his face. He looks older, more mature, a fully developed man. And amazingly, now that I see Chad's face, I can look at other moments in my mind and see him clearly.

I touch the photo, wishing I could touch him, praying I will get to hug my big brother, who I thought buried beneath fire and pain. The photo feeds my hope. There's another photo of him on a motorcycle, and my mind replays the many times I saw him on one in Egypt. And there's one more of him with Meg, his arm around her shoulder. I try to see the spark between them that I know people must see between me and Liam, but it's not there. Maybe if he was looking at her, I'd see it.

The announcements for landing begin, and I glance at Meg. "Thank you."

"You can keep them. I have more."

"Thank you." I tuck the photos into my purse, when I'd really like to study them longer, but I need to mentally prepare myself for what might be waiting at the gate when we land. Or rather, who.

By the time we exit the plane in Austin I'm a ball of nerves, and having Meg holding my arm like she's afraid someone will grab me and run doesn't help. Clearing the Jetway, I scan the crowd, and a mix of disappointment and relief washes over me when my big, bossy, lovable man is nowhere to be found.

"So far, so good," Meg murmurs. "Let's hope that means your plan worked."

"Yes. Let's hope." And I do. This is a miserable way to operate, but it's about protecting the two men I'm blessed to have alive and well.

Moving through the airport to the rental car shuttle, despite all the reasons Liam's absence is a good thing, I crave the sense of awareness I have when he's nearby, that odd prickling of my skin and the singing of my soul that he creates. But it doesn't come. He isn't here.

By the time we exit the shuttle van to pick up our rental car, the warm Texas November has me tying my jacket at my waist, and fairly confident that we aren't looking at any roadblocks of a Liam Stone nature. Once we're settled in a gray Dodge, we pull onto Interstate 35 for the half-hour drive to Jasmine Heights. I sink down into the seat and ball my fists on my legs. I'm going to face the Godzillas of my past without Liam.

"At least it's a short drive," Meg comments. "Thirty minutes, according to the GPS." She pauses and looks at me. "You okay?"

I don't look at her. "Yes."

She's quiet a moment. I want her to stay that way. She doesn't. "You think they'll kill him if we don't jog your memory in Jasmine Heights?"

My windpipe tightens and I force out a reply. "I think they'll hurt him, or someone else I care about."

"Like Liam."

"Yes." The word is lead on my tongue. "Like Liam."

We fall into blessed silence and I stare straight ahead, willing myself to be calm and collected. I'm terrified that the answer to all of this isn't in my head—or if it is, that I won't remember it in time to save Chad and Liam. I can't lose my brother when I've just found him again. And I can't lose the man who brought me back to life. But my track record of love and loss is terrifying.

"Jasmine Heights city limits," Meg finally announces, and I sit up straight, staring at the sign I thought I'd never see again. She asks, "Any hotel preference?"

"I don't know." I don't care. "Stay on this road and take

the Snyder exit." After the exit, I direct her through several twists and turns. "Here," I say at the final turn, and frown at the new shopping center in my old neighborhood.

"This isn't a hotel."

"No. It's my old house." But now it's a restaurant. My house is a restaurant. "Pull into the driveway."

"Shouldn't we get a motel first?"

"Pull in, Meg," I bite out.

"Fine. I'll pull in."

She parks in the front row of spaces, to the right of the door. I stare at the fancy red-and-white brick building, with a big sign that reads "Red Heaven Restaurant." The irony of the *heaven* doesn't escape me. Though the population of this city has grown from ten thousand to nearly twenty since I was last here, it was, and is, still small enough that everyone knows what happened here.

"Red Heaven," I whisper.

"Did you want to go in and eat?" Meg asks.

Customers are sitting at a table that might be on the same spot where my mother screamed as she burned alive. "Evil," I say.

"What? The food is evil? That's a new one." I don't speak to her. I can't speak to her. My gaze goes back to the sign. It's an insult; a battle cry, and a threat. I expect pain and a flashback that takes me down. Instead, there's a burning in my chest and tension in my shoulders. My jaw clenches and I shove open the car door.

"I guess we're going to eat evil food," Meg mumbles, but I ignore her.

On the way to the entrance, I fix my bag crossbody over my chest. Pushing open the door, I'm in a homey restaurant with hardwood floors and wooden tables with comfy chairs. *Homey* being the operative word—like the home it once was.

"Who owns this place?" I ask the twentysomething girl behind the wooden hostess stand. Oh, God—I think she's the kid I used to babysit a few blocks from here.

Her dark brown brows knit. "Do I know you?"

"No, you don't. I need the name of the owner."

"Sheridan Scott. He owns everything around here."

As Derek had said. "Do you have a business card for him?"

"The manager might. She's behind the bar right now."

"Did we get a table?" Meg asks.

A shiver of unease slides down my spine, and the source seems to be Meg. My nerves are jumping and my mood is suited for a tornadic event, and I don't try to understand it. "I'm going to the bathroom." I start walking, praying she won't follow. I intend to head to the bar afterward, and I don't want Meg to join me.

I push open the door to the bathroom, thankful it's made for one. When I turn to lock up a man shoves his way inside, giving me his back, his long, light brown hair tied at the nape of his neck, while he locks the door himself.

My heart races and my hand goes to my purse, but he's turned before I can make a move. And though I'd once thought him the epitome of rugged bad-boy hotness, I know better now. He's danger in a way Liam never was.

I clutch the strap of my purse. "What are you doing here, Jared?"

"I have a message from Chad."

I blanch, but for some reason I'm not shocked. I think I always knew Jared was more than just my next-door neighbor in Denver. "Let me see your tattoo."

"I'm not a part of your brother's underground society, but I think the message will clear up any trust issues." He sets his phone on the counter, then pushes Play on a voice mail.

Jared, it's Chad.

At the sound of my brother's voice, the air rushes from my lungs and tears burn my eyes. *He's alive.* Deep down, part of me hadn't allowed myself to really believe it was true.

You were right on the ping on Lara, the voice mail continues. *I moved her to Denver as we'd planned, but there's trouble.*

I have to make arrangements. I need you to come here and look out for her for a couple of weeks. Fuck. I have to go. I need you here. I have to protect my sister, man.

And there it is. Proof that Chad has been alive all these years, and an explanation as to why Jared felt so familiar. On some soul-deep level, I think Chad must be the cause of that odd attachment I felt to Jared in Denver.

"Tell me I haven't lost him before I find him again." My voice quakes, the fear digging a hole in my already bleeding heart.

"I don't know where he is, but I promise you, I'm trying my damnedest to find him."

"Not the answer I want." My throat is raw and scratchy.

"It's the only one I have to give."

I hate that reply, as much as Liam must have when I used it on him. "What did he mean by *ping*?"

"I'm a tech expert. A hacker, but legit now. I use those skills to monitor internet chatter that involves you or your brother, and set up pings or notifications if a match occurs. But I wasn't the only one watching you. When you went to work at the museum, someone had a wide search set up that fit the profile of your employment, which triggered a ping."

"So *I* did this? I made this hell start all over?" I don't know why I'm asking. I know I'm responsible.

"No, you didn't do this. Chad did—but I think you know that."

"I know nothing. *Nothing*. I'm living on the run, and I didn't even know that my own brother was alive!"

Suddenly I'm against the wall and he's in front of me. "Shhh. You have to be quiet."

"I have to do a *lot* of things. Hide. Change my name. Lie. I have to lie a lot. Don't lie to me, Jared."

"Sweetheart—"

"And don't call me 'sweetheart,' or even Lara. I'm Amy and I'm staying Amy, and you'd better not be here to tell me I'm Mary or Casey or Sandy. I'm *Amy*."

He stares at me for several beats and says, "Amy. I didn't come here to change your name. I came to save your life— and Chad's, I hope like hell, while I'm at it."

"How do you know him? Why do you care?"

He pushes off the wall and leans on the sink, his face turning all hard lines and shadows, like he doesn't like the story he has to tell. "Back when we were at UT together, my sister was dying of cancer and the insurance wasn't paying for all of the treatments. I started hacking computers for money, and Chad knew about it. What *I* didn't know was that he was in deep with some powerful assholes from doing some of his own dirty work."

"What kind of dirty work?"

"Oil guys is all I know. Your dad got involved, and got nervous. Chad took over and formed his underground of followers. My sister had no one but me, so I didn't want to know more—and he didn't offer."

My stomach roils with the memory of the stranger handing my father the envelope. What Jared's saying adds up, and it feels right.

"Chad needed a job done," he continues, "and it paid four times as much as any job I'd done. He knew I'd keep my mouth shut, and I trusted him to keep me out of his dirty business." His voice tightens. "My sister had five more years because I did that job, and Chad and I lost contact. Until the fire. He needed to make you both disappear. And like your brother did for my sister, I became your guardian angel."

"And the man who brought me the paperwork and money to disappear with from the hospital?"

"No idea. I just created your identity."

"And Meg?"

"Meg." His voice bites on her name.

"She says she's Chad's wife."

He snorts. "I've never heard about a wife. I've only talked to him three times in six years, but I didn't hear him asking me to protect any *wife* on that message. And Chad isn't someone to turn his back on a responsibility, even if the love was gone. He'd protect those who count on him to the death."

"Yes. He would."

"I also don't think a wife would be sticking her tongue down some guy's throat when she thinks her husband is missing—would you?"

"What? What guy?"

He punches a button on his phone and hands it to me, showing a photo of her in an embrace with a man twenty-plus years her senior. And I don't need a forward shot to know that he's the same man who'd been with my mother and arguing with my father. "Who is he?" I look at him urgently. "Who *is* he?"

"You've seen him before."

"Yeah. Arguing with my father, then my brother, and sticking his tongue down my mother's throat."

His gaze sharpens. "Sounds like we have a lot to chat with Meg about, doesn't it?"

"Yes, we do." But I barely get the declaration out for the splintering in my brain. I sway, and Jared closes the distance between us and grabs me. "Whoa. Easy there, sweetheart. You okay?"

"God, I hate that word." I suck in a breath, resting my head on his chest and curling my fingers around his shirt. "But yes. Okay. Give me . . . a minute. Or . . . two . . ." Prickling begins in my head and I both welcome it for the memory I need to embrace and curse the timing.

"Amy?"

At the sound of Meg's voice, my head jerks up, sending shooting pain through my skull.

Jared presses a finger to my mouth in silent warning.

I nod, my mind racing. "Yes," I call out. "I'm sick again. Can you get me a ginger ale, please?"

"Oh. Sure. Be right back." Her footsteps fade.

His hands close on my shoulders, too intimate, too like the way only Liam should touch me. It's not exactly wrong without being right. "We need to move now," he says. "Are you able to?"

"I'm fine. It's just—"

"Blood sugar," he supplies, reminding me of the excuse I've used with him in the past. "Right. Heard that before. The only reason I haven't grabbed Meg and forced the bitch to talk was that I wanted to talk to you first. I needed you to trust me. And though I don't want you with that woman any longer than you have to be, we need to get her alone. Go with her to a hotel. I'll follow."

"And then?"

"We get the answer to where the hell Chad is."

"You think she knows?"

"She seems to know a hell of a lot more than either of us."

"Yes, she does," I say bitterly, and the idea that Meg has

played a role in hurting my brother seems to have shaken my flashback completely, leaving me with one goal on my mind; exposing what's in her head, not mine.

"The sooner we do this, the better."

Jared steps away from me, leaving me suddenly aware that his legs have been pressed way too snugly against mine.

He knows, too. It's in the air around us, wrapping us in an awareness that has me cutting my gaze and turning to the door. His hand comes down on my shoulder, and I do not feel the liquid heat Liam's touch creates in me, but one hand stays on my shoulder and I feel warmth and strength. "If you feel threatened at all, get the hell away from her. I'll have your back. Like Chad had mine."

Emotion I can't afford to feel wells in my chest, and I reach for the door, unlocking it and pulling it open. Then I exit, leaving my new protector behind. I don't doubt Jared. I never did.

I enter the restaurant, scanning for Meg, but I don't see her. From the corner of my eye I see the front door swing shut, and I take off running. Bursting through the doors, I have just enough time to see the rental car disappearing down the street.

A white truck pulls up next to me and the passenger door pops open. "Get in," Jared orders.

I climb inside, but it's too late. Meg is gone.

SEVENTEEN

"NOW WHAT?" I ASK AS JARED pulls the truck onto the road.

"Now we regroup," he replies, and I can feel the probing look he gives me though his eyes should be on the road. "How did you end up with Meg?"

"How did you find me?"

"I hacked my way to nothing. You'd clearly dumped your cell phone, because it wouldn't ping, so—"

"You had my cell phone pinged?"

"Hacker, sweetheart. Of course I did."

I remember the mysterious call I'd received. "*You* called my cell phone?"

"Liam had several lines. I had to make sure it was yours."

"You scared the crap out of me."

"Sorry, not my intent. And speaking of scaring the crap out of someone, what the hell were you thinking, using the Amy Bensen ID to fly? That's how I found you. And I guarantee you it's how others will, too."

I don't explain. I'm not done asking questions. "And how did you get here this fast?"

"I was already back in Texas."

"And Meg? Where has she been?"

"She disappeared when you did." He pulls into a motel parking lot a few blocks from the restaurant that used to be my home. "This place isn't Liam Stone–quality, but it has beds."

I grimace at the disdain in his voice when he says Liam's name, and as much as I trust and love Liam, my brother's worry over him worries me. "What's your problem with Liam?"

"Money. Money, and, let me think—oh, yeah. More money."

"Why is money a problem?" I ask, though that's exactly what worried me about Liam in the past.

"Chad was in bed with an enemy with bucketloads of

money. Liam has bucketloads of money, and those people don't grow on trees. It's a common denominator, and it's dangerous."

"He's not dangerous to me or my brother. He's dangerous to anyone who tries to hurt me."

"If you trust him, then why leave him behind in Denver?"

"How do you know I wasn't with him?"

"Hacking has a broad reach. He was looking for you, just like I was."

"I got spooked."

"Stay spooked. It's safer, where he's concerned. And he's going to get that same ID flag I did. If I'm right about him, and he's in this mess up to his neck, he's going to come for you—and we're going to need a plan, soon."

He clearly doesn't know I've reunited with Liam, and I'm not telling him. "Did my brother say Liam was a part of this?"

"I'd love to lie and get you the hell out from under Liam's spell. I thought you were, but you clearly aren't. But you were right when you said you've lived enough lies. I haven't had any conversations with your brother about Liam Stone. But I don't like that when I got to Denver, Chad wasn't there and Liam was."

"Do you have one piece of information, in all your hacking or otherwise, that says he's part of this?"

"No, but—"

"No," I supply. "That's the answer. And yes, he has money. That isn't a sin."

"Do you trust me?"

"I don't know you. I'm with you because my brother trusts you."

"If Liam Stone wants whatever Chad has, he will come for you. If Liam Stone wants you, he will come for you. Either way, we have him to deal with. And Meg, who you still haven't told me how you ended up with." He scrubs a hand over his jaw and sighs. "Right now we need to get inside, where we'll feel safer. I'm going in to register, and I'd rather you not be seen, but I don't want you sitting here unprotected." He reaches across me, his arm touching my leg as he opens the glove compartment and then sets a gun on the seat between us. "I'll be as quick as I can. I know you know how to shoot. Chad talked about you a lot. It's loaded, so lock up until I get back, and shoot anyone who isn't me that tries to get in the truck. I'd say 'including Liam Stone,' but I don't think you'd listen."

As he starts to leave I call, "Aren't you afraid I'll take off?"

"You want to save your brother. I want to save your brother. No. I don't think you'll take off."

Then he's gone, leaving me wondering what he has to

show me—which I'm certain was his intent. I watch him enter the motel, all loose-legged swagger and bad-boy confidence—a different kind of male grace than Liam's, but still a demanding presence. Though he looks nothing like Chad, he reminds me of him, and I can see them as friends.

I settle the gun in my lap, check the safety, and spend the next five minutes scanning the area, intermittently eyeing Jared through the glass at the counter. I'm surprised to find myself calm and unemotional. I'm in that zone I use to survive. It used to be my comfort zone, a place where I escaped the darkness of my fear, but now it's an icy, hollow place I don't want to visit.

In a few minutes, Jared saunters back toward me and climbs into the truck, surprising me by reaching for the gun in my lap, covering my hand that holds it with his.

Our eyes meet and I can see the heat in his, and I'm not sure why. I'm a mess, barely showered and . . . I just don't get it, but I'm hoping it's not going to be a problem.

"I'll let you keep it on one condition," he negotiates.

"Condition?"

"You have to promise not to use it on me."

"Haven't considered that just yet."

He chuckles and sits back to start the engine. "Guess I'm doing something right, then. Put it in your purse. I'll feel better if you're armed. We're around the back of the building. I didn't want us to be seen, and the faster we get inside and stay inside, the better."

The familiar drill, and supposed brilliance, of the hermit strategy. Until there's a fire. It's a horrible thought, and I cut my gaze to the window, thinking of that damned sign: Red Heaven Restaurant. Maybe it's a tribute, not a slap, but Sheridan is into oil, and thanks to Jared, I now know my family was, too.

He opens his door and I blink when I realize he's killed the engine. I quickly place the gun in my purse and follow him outside, surprised at how little anxiety I feel with Jared, considering the motel we find ourselves in. But he knows my brother, and I hunger to hear more about Chad. Even more, I crave the moment when I can hug my brother again.

By the time I read the number on the chipped powder blue door, Jared is already swiping the key. He motions me forward and I'm relieved to find two beds, which seem to support my trust in Jared. Or maybe it's all the place had, but I'm going to go with my instincts.

Jared shuts the door and locks it, then unzips his bag and sets a gun on a bed. Now I'm nervous and my heart lurches, my eyes meeting his. "If anyone comes in that door," he says, motioning to the gun, "they meet Berta. And she's a bitch to swallow."

"Well then, I'm glad to meet her," I say, though she isn't

any more comforting than his obvious assumption that we need her.

His eyes soften, his voice turning gentle. "Why don't you sit down, so we can talk."

I nod and claim the opposite bed, and we sit with the nightstand separating us, knees a foot apart. He just stares at me, and I don't like the sympathy etched in his brown eyes.

"Whatever you're not saying, just say it. You're scaring me again."

He nods. "All right—I'm going to get right to what matters. Four days after I got the message from your brother, I got a second call from him. This time, I answered in time to talk to him."

Adrenaline pours through me. "Why didn't you tell me sooner?"

"It wasn't the right time."

I'm pretty sure that means I'm not going to like what is coming. "And?" I prod anxiously.

"I'm going to shoot straight with you, because I think it's the only way you can make a clear decision about what comes next."

I clutch the blanket on the bed. "What does that mean?"

"It means Chad was desperate, and whispering on the call, clearly hiding. He said . . . he said he wasn't going to make it through the night, and all he cared about was protecting you."

"No. No. That can't be. You said—"

"I haven't given up hope on him. He was calling me to ensure you survived. He's a survivor, too, though, Amy. We'll fight for him. I promise you."

Hope is my enemy. It's worse than lies. It promises and then it takes back. It teases and then it rips my heart out. "What else did he say?"

"He told me he left you instructions to protect yourself, and that one hundred eleven is the way to do it—whatever that means."

"One hundred eleven," I murmur. At first I think of the locker number at JFK where he'd left me a note, but then another memory surfaces. He and I had been at a dig site in Egypt, hanging out in a tent as we often did, and Chad was stuffing pieces of paper he'd written on in an old wine bottle.

"What's that?" I ask.

"One hundred reasons why, and eleven assholes."

"What does that mean?"

"Nothing I ever want you to understand."

"Do you know what it means?" Jared asks.

"It's his lucky number." I know what it means, and where to find it. "He used it for a lot of things. What else?"

"He told me to tell you he's sorry this hell happened, and he knows you can never forgive him, but he loves you. Then the line went dead."

My breath hitches and I lower my head, pressing my hand to my forehead. I've lost him before I even found him again. No. No. *No*.

I push to my feet and start for the door.

Jared grabs my arm. "Whoa. Where are you going?"

"Meg said they have my brother. They gave me four days to get them what they want, or they'll kill him. Maybe one hundred eleven is what they want. I have to go now."

"You know what he was telling you with one hundred eleven?"

"Yes." I tug on my arm. "We need to go *now*."

He doesn't budge. "Who are 'they,' and how did 'they' contact you?"

"I don't know who 'they' are. The man in the photo, oil people, the Underground—it could be any of them. And I don't even care. I just want to know what one hundred eleven tells me before they kill him."

"How do you know they plan to kill him?"

"Meg showed me a note and a text message. That's how she got me to go with her. So I have to figure out what they want."

"We need to think before we act. They'll be watching.

They could take whatever you're after from you, and still kill him."

"If they haven't already."

"They won't kill him if they think he's the way to motivate you to give them what they want. And they won't kill you if they think you know what that is. Chad isn't a fool. He knows how to spin information."

I shove his chest. "We can't just stand here. What I'm thinking of might not even be what they want. I have to go get it—there's no time!"

"I just told you: they aren't going to kill him if they think you have what they want."

"You don't even know who 'they' are or what they want so you can't be sure of that!"

A knock sounds on the door, and Liam's voice calls, "Amy!"

My heart lurches, and a mix of dread and absolute happiness fills me.

Jared pulls me to him, keeping me grounded in the reality of my life and the hell I live in. "What 'they' might do is kill lover boy out there as an example, and leave Chad alive. Get rid of him. Tell him you're fucking me. Tell him that you used him for money to save your brother. Whatever you have to say, get rid of him. And if you can't, be worried that he's one of them. Understand?"

"Yes. Yes, you're right."

He studies me a moment, his stare probing, then gently pushes me away from him, reaching for Berta. "Why do you need that?" I ask.

"Amy, damn it, open up," Liam shouts.

Ignoring the demand, Jared answers me. "Making sure neither of us ends up dead." Then he walks toward the door. There's a grace and comfort to the way he handles the weapon that suggests experience. Lots of experience. He's far more than a hacker, and I suddenly want to warn Liam.

I turn for my purse, intending to reach for my weapon, but I never get the chance. Jared unlocks the door, it bursts open. Tellar stalks into the room, his gun pointed at Jared.

I blink and Tellar and Jared are split at the foot of each bed, each stiff-armed and pointing a weapon at the other. Watching them, I back against the nightstand. But then Liam steps into the room, and I see no one but him. Since the first night I met him he's oozed money, power, and sex, but he's so much more to me now. He is compassion, trust . . . love.

His eyes land on me, and I see the terror he's felt for me, and his relief that I'm here and safe. He steps toward me, and I toward him.

Jared shouts, "Go anywhere near her and I'll shoot your buddy here!"

Liam freezes, and Tellar promises, "You'll take a fucking bullet doing it."

I glance between them, the long-haired renegade and the bulkier, buzz-cut military man, both with jaws set, both with steady hands, both clearly willing to pull the trigger.

"Amy," Liam says softly, easily commanding my attention.

A storm erupts inside me. I love him. I love him with all my heart, and I cannot let him die. I won't let him die.

"Go away, Liam," I force myself to say. "I'm not with you anymore. I'm with Jared. I was always with Jared."

"You don't really expect me to believe that, do you?"

"It was about your money," I say, but the words are lead on my tongue. "I needed it to get to my brother, but it's handled. He's safe, and you and your arrogant self can just go away."

His gaze slips to Jared and back to me. "So you're fucking him?"

"I . . . yes. Yes, I am."

"While you're pregnant with my child."

I ignore Jared's curse at the surprising news and stay focused on Liam. "Why do you think I was so pissed when you didn't use a condom?"

I've hit a nerve, and anger hardens his handsome face.

"Whatever you're doing, stop." His voice is ice, laced with pain, and it's just too much. This is *all* too much.

I hurt. I don't want Liam to hurt. Regret shakes me to the core, and suddenly I don't know what insanity made me listen to Jared. There's only one way to handle Liam, and this isn't it.

I grab my purse, pulling the gun from inside. Liam doesn't move. He stands there, unmoving, unreadable. I point the gun at Tellar, and then Jared. "Both of you get out."

Tellar curses, and Jared flicks me a shocked look. "Amy—"

"I won't kill either of you, but I'll shoot you in the legs and knock some of the damned testosterone out of you. Now get out! Fight outside. You figure it out, and let us figure it out."

"Get out, Tellar," Liam orders softly.

Both men hesitate, and seem to come to a silent understanding. Then they harness their weapons and head for the door. It shuts behind them, leaving Liam and me alone.

EIGHTEEN

LIAM JUST STANDS THERE, LOOKING GOOD enough to lick and mad enough to tear down the walls of the dingy motel. He owns me, and I can't do anything about it. I don't even want to try, yet the hell of my life keeps forcing me to push him away.

The gun shakes in my hand. "I told you not to get killed. Charging in here is not the way to stay alive."

He advances on me slowly, and each step is like a band stretching around us, ready to snap at any moment. I'm not sure what to expect when it does. "And holding a gun on me makes sense in this equation how?"

"Everything isn't an equation. It just . . . is."

"Like me coming for you?" He stops in front of me and closes his hand over mine on the gun, but it is nothing like that earlier moment. I gasp as the sensations rush over me, and I have this undeniable sense of us being two parts of one whole. Of not fully breathing while we were apart. "You had to know I wasn't going to leave you in a motel room with Jared." There's intensity in his tone, and in his eyes there's a promise that I am his and he'll never let me go. That I am as rooted in his soul as he is in mine, and he's going to fight for what that means, while I'm fighting to save his life.

"I told you to go to Denver," I whisper.

"I sent Derek."

"What if I was in Denver?"

"You aren't."

Electricity charges the air, and the tension between us jolts up another notch. "You didn't know I wouldn't be."

"Yes, I did. And while I was in the air traveling here, I got the alert that you were headed here, too."

"From my ID at the airport," I say. "And I went straight to my old house. I made it easy for anyone to find me."

He gives a nod of confirmation. "You wanted me to find you."

Yes. "No. I wanted to find you when this was over."

"Together, baby. We've talked about this." He sets the gun on the bed, and I swear the few seconds he isn't touching me are hell. His hands come down on my shoulders. "Do you know how much what you said about Jared killed me, after I'd already died a million deaths in the past twenty-four hours?"

My heart squeezes with the vulnerability of his confession, the intensity of his tone, and I wrap my arms around him, absorbing the heat of his body, the power and strength. "I didn't mean anything I said. I hated it. But . . ."

I look up at him, urgency roaring to life in me. "They'll *kill* you. You have to leave. Go underground—please. I'm begging you, Liam. Go underground, like you wanted me to. They won't kill me. Not when they think I have what they want."

His hands slip into my hair. "I'm not going anywhere without you. I leave when you leave. And you're not going anywhere with Jared."

His mouth comes down on mine, and it's pain and heartache, but there's more. There is a harder edge, a demand, anger.

I'm angry, too, and I don't think it's at him. I just am, and so is he, and we're all over each other, wildly kissing, tugging at clothes. My shirt is tossed to the floor and I shove his up his torso, seeking skin against skin, no barriers, at a time when there seem to be too many between us.

My hand covers his pi tattoo, where I want my mouth to be, but as he's unhooking my bra I hear the rumble of the men arguing outside. I grab it, holding it in place. "We can't. Tellar and Jared."

"Ask me if I care about them right now." He tugs the bra away, pulling my mouth to his again. "You said you fucked Jared."

I forget my hesitation of moments before. "I told you, I was trying to scare you away. You know that."

"That didn't make it easy to hear. That doesn't stop the burning inside me that says I need to remind you who you belong with."

"I don't need a reminder."

"I think you do." He lifts me and carries me to the bed, setting me on the mattress. My shoes and jeans, and even my panties, are gone before I can protest. Not that I want to. For as much as I hate that I've made him feel he needs to prove something, the fierce, intense, dominant man he is now calls to me. Liam speaks to me on some level beyond words, like an expression of something I have inside me, and that I find within him.

He drags me to the end of the bed and turns me onto my stomach, his hands going to my hips to pull me onto my knees. I'm submissive to him like this, and I think I understand him more now than I ever have. He needs the control he's felt he'd lost the past few days. And the truth is, I need to give it to him. He's my escape, the only place I can let go, the only person I can trust.

He leans down and cradles my body, caresses my breasts, brushing my hair off my back so that the long, blond strands fall to the bed, blocking my vision. But I don't need to see. That's what is so erotic, so perfect, with Liam. I truly trust him.

His lips settle at the nape of my neck, his hand kneading my breast, teasing my nipple. My breasts are heavy, my sex aching, my thighs damp. He kisses between my shoulder blades, then flattens his palm there, slowly dragging his hand down my back to cup my backside.

He'd once threatened to spank me, and the memory is confusingly erotic, teasingly sensational. But he doesn't now, and somehow I knew he wouldn't. He cups my cheeks, and then caresses down my thighs and back up. His fingers slip intimately between my legs, into the slickness of my swollen, aroused body, and I fall to my elbows, unable to hold myself up on my hands.

He begins to stroke me, playing with my clit, and then slips two fingers inside me, filling me, stretching me. I find myself leaning back into the touch, arching my back, pushing for more. I know he could take me over the edge, but he doesn't. He teases me. Pulling his fingers out. Pressing them back inside me. Repeating until I think I'll go crazy. Finally, oh yes, finally, he takes me to that edge, and I'm ready. So very ready, when suddenly his fingers are gone, and I'm panting in agony.

He places his hand on my back and leans over me, his mouth moving to my ear. "Not without me. Not this time. You need to remember the meaning of 'together.' Don't move."

Don't move. Easier said than done, but I can hear him undressing, and I focus on the idea of him being inside me. How good it will feel when that first touch of his cock becomes a deep push. And I get what I crave.

His hands come down on my hips. His shaft settles between my thighs. "Mine," he growls, and he thrusts into me, driving hard and deep.

I moan and expect another thrust, but instead he goes down on the bed and pulls my back to his chest, his hand covering my breast. His lips are at my ear as he whispers, "Mine."

"Yes. Yours."

"He wants to fuck you." He tugs erotically on my nipple, as if he's punishing me with pleasure, his hips grinding into me.

"And I want to fuck *you*," I pant.

He pulls out of me and turns me to face him, presses his cock inside me and cups my backside to bury himself deep inside me again. We lie there, our eyes connecting, as he murmurs, "The best fucking, baby, is when it's—"

"Raw and honest," I whisper.

His sensual mouth curves slightly. "And when it's wicked hot and driven by love." His fingers settle on my face. "Like I love you—with everything I am and ever will be."

He loves me. I knew it, but hearing it is everything. "I love you, too. I didn't want to tell you in a note, but I didn't want to risk never telling you at all."

"I know," he murmurs, pressing my back to mold my chest to his. "Don't ever leave me again."

It's an order, but somewhere in the depth of the command is a plea, and pain. I hear the pain etched in his words, see it in his eyes. Not for the first time, I am struck by the way we speak to each other beyond words. The way my soul knows his soul. Love and loss have touched our lives, but with all his money and power, he has never felt what family truly means. He has never felt that unity and peace.

I twine my fingers in his dark hair. "You have to know that leaving you was about not losing you. Please tell me you know that."

"I do know. But I can't go through that again, Amy.

Together means *together*. Whatever happens, you come to me and we'll handle it."

"I just—"

He cups my head and kisses me. "No excuses. Together. That's what you say you want."

"It is."

"No exceptions."

"No exceptions," I murmur, and his tongue sweeps against mine, tender and sweet, and where I've tasted possession and need in him in the past, I taste love and heartache now. I moan and deepen the kiss, trying to wash away the hurt in him I know runs deeper than me and this moment in time. It's why he understands mine.

I don't know when we start moving. We just do, and it is passion and pleasure and absolute perfection in the midst of the danger surrounding us. All that matters are these moments, and every touch, every lick, every move, is about the forever we want to share together. The family we want to be together. I want it to last, but too soon I tumble into those blissful spasms of release and he shudders with his own. It is truly bittersweet.

In the aftermath we hold each other, neither of us caring about the stickiness on our thighs, or the two men outside the room. We lie there together, breathing. Eventually Liam pulls out of me and walks to the bathroom, returning with a towel, helping me clean myself up, and it doesn't make me blush. It somehow makes me feel closer to him.

We lie on our backs and stare at the stained ceiling. "Is the house okay?" I ask.

"It's fine, but even if it wasn't, it can be replaced." He turns to look at me. "You can't."

I roll to my side to face him. "I wouldn't have been able to forgive myself if Alex's home had been destroyed."

"I told you—"

I touch his lips. "I know. You're worried about me, but what is important to you is important to me." I think of Meg's claim that she'd set the fire, but now it seems like it must have been done with help. "Was there a bomb?"

"No bomb."

I let out a breath. "That's a relief."

"How did you end up with Jared instead of Meg?"

"When I got here, I went to my old house—"

"Red Heaven Restaurant," he supplies.

A burn starts in my chest. "You know?"

"Derek figured it out after he put Sheridan Scott on the radar." He takes my hand. "I should have been there when you found out."

"I know you wanted to be, and that's enough." I lower my lashes a moment, reining in my emotions before I look at him again. "It feels like a slap."

"It's meant as one."

"So you think he's involved."

"Yes. I have no proof, but I'll get it. What happened to Meg?"

"Jared showed up at the restaurant and she took off."

"Interesting. I've been checking on her."

"And?"

"Her identity is just a shell, like yours."

This doesn't surprise me. "She says she's Chad's wife."

"Nothing in any of the data on her suggests she's married to anyone, let alone Chad."

"Jared seemed surprised, too, when I told him, especially since Chad didn't mention her. He has a picture of her with the man from the black sedan who was with my mother."

Liam scrubs his jaw. "There's one from left field. I didn't expect that. Does he know who the man is?"

"No. He's just this perpetual mystery we can't solve."

He studies me with hooded eyes, several seconds ticking by. "About Jared—"

"I'd been with him all of an hour. He tracked me using my ID, just like you did."

"Why is he involved in this?"

"He's an old friend of my brother's." I detail everything Jared shared with me.

"You believe him?" Liam asks, sounding skeptical.

"He had a voice mail from my brother begging him to protect me. I heard it, Liam. He'll play it for you."

"So your brother's . . . alive."

"Yes. Or he was. All these years, he's been alive and living a few blocks from me. But now—" *Meg is gone.* "Oh, God."

I sit up and Liam follows. "What is it, Amy?"

"Meg was my connection to whoever has Chad. I was so taken aback by Chad's voice mail, I forgot how important her link to my brother is!" I scramble off the bed, then cringe as I'm hit with cramps.

"Amy." Liam is by my side in an instant, his arms around me. "Easy, baby. What's wrong?"

I swallow hard and straighten. "I'm fine. It's over. Just some cramps. From the sex, I think."

His brows furrow. "Is that normal?"

"I don't know."

"I'll call Dr. Murphy."

I grab his arm, feeling the urgency of saving my brother's life. "Not yet. Not now. My brother left me a message with Jared. He said he wasn't going to make it through the night, but to tell me one hundred eleven was the way to protect myself. I hope it's also what these people want, so we can get him back. I hope he's still alive."

"What's one hundred eleven?"

"On a dig, he was doing this 'message in a bottle' thing where he wrote notes and stuffed them inside it. I asked him what it was, and he said 'one hundred reasons why, and eleven assholes.' "

"What does that mean?"

"I asked that, and he said he hoped I never had to find out."

"His backup plan. Where is it?"

"My senior year, right before the fire, my gym class buried a time capsule at school, to be opened in twenty years. My brother brought that bottle and put it inside."

"Then we need to go dig up the time capsule. Right after we deal with Jared."

NINETEEN

IT'S TEN O'CLOCK AT NIGHT WHEN we reach the back of my old high school, near the site of the buried time capsule. Tellar does the dirty work while Liam, Jared, and I beam our flashlights on the site. Thankfully, the building hides us from the main road. The capsule is buried close to the surface, and the shovel clangs against metal in just five minutes.

Tellar dusts off the big steel box, and we squat around him as he lifts the lid. Anxiously, I dig through the various items placed inside, relieved when I spot the bottle. "Thank

God," I whisper, removing it and hugging it to me. "Please let this be the ticket to saving Chad."

Liam strokes my hair behind my ear. "Let's hope, baby."

Tellar shuts the lid and refills the hole, and we kill our flashlights to make the dark trek back to Liam's rental, a massive Land Rover. Tellar and Jared pile in the front of the vehicle and Liam and I claim the back. I immediately uncork the bottle and start trying to remove the paper stashed inside.

"We should wait until we get to the motel," Liam warns, having arranged a nicer place for us to stay up the road that he says is safer. All I care is that it's farther from my old home. Being near it is harder than I'd thought it would be.

But I'm not prepared to wait. "I need to know if what's inside can save my brother." I finally pull out several pieces of paper from the narrow mouth of the bottle.

Liam curses and Tellar locks the doors with a grumble of, "I guess we're doing this now."

Obviously caving to my urgency, Liam shines his flashlight over one piece of paper after another. They tell me nothing, and I turn to him. "What do you make of it?"

"Names, dates, and types of transactions. And the details are clear. They're all illegal."

"That doesn't surprise me," Jared says. "Powerful men believe they can get away with anything."

Liam arches a brow.

"Some powerful men," Jared amends. "And the jury is still out on you."

"How are the crimes tied to Chad?" Tellar asks, ignoring the exchange.

I unroll another piece of paper and see a list of names, with Sheridan Scott's at the top. I show it to Liam. "The eleven assholes."

"What?" Jared and Tellar ask at the same time.

"When my brother was filling the bottle, he said there were a hundred reasons 'why,' whatever that means, and eleven assholes. These are the names of the eleven assholes."

"Rich assholes," Jared adds.

Liam glances at the list and hands it to Jared. "Anyone else you know on it?"

Jared gives it a once-over. "I hacked for number three. Don't know the rest."

Tellar surveys the names next. "No one from our research, but I'll get Derek to run it through the FBI system."

"Don't," Jared warns. "It could trigger alerts we don't want with law enforcement. Chad would rather be dead in jail, I promise you."

I remove a larger piece of paper that says *Lara*, and show it to Liam. His hand slides to my leg and he leans in as I unroll it, shining the light on it and reading it with me.

Lara,

If you're reading this, everything
has gone terribly wrong. I just hope
things aren't as bad as I've imagined
they could be. It all started with
creative fundraising. Dad and I
wanted to work certain sites, and it
wasn't happening financially. That led
us to a group called The Underground-
treasure hunters all over the world,
each with their own leadership.
Someone wants something and the
price is right, so we get it for them
and ask as few questions as possible.
I got greedy. The money . . . I hope
like hell you never read this and
know the way I've let it control me.

I took jobs I shouldn't have, ones
off the grid of the Underground.
And one of those treasures is
something I can't hand over. It
would cost too many lives, and I
know you can't live with innocent
people dying, any more than I can.

The Underground is working on how to protect me and our family, even as I write this. But I can't take the chance that I end up dead and they don't protect you.

Copy the list of names and the one hundred crimes I've included. Then tear the list in half to show only the first five names. March into Sheridan Scott's office and tell him if you or anyone you need to protect ends up dead, you've arranged to have the rest of the list and the documentation I've provided mailed directly to the Travis County district attorney, the FBI, the CIA, and local law enforcement. You have to go in person. Look him in the eyes and make sure he sees no fear. I know how the man operates, and this will ensure he really takes care of it himself.

This is my fault, Lara, and I'm sorry. I love you, and I love Mom *and Dad. I would never do anything to hurt you, and it kills me to know that I can't just make this go away.*

Chad

His words stab me in the heart a million times over. The bottle doesn't save him. It saves me. And I wait for some kind of meltdown, but it doesn't come. It's there, though, simmering in a hole inside me that was carved with what I thought was his death.

In this instant, I go into my zone, that place my mind takes me when I'm right up against survival. I hand the note to Jared and calmly start rolling all the papers up.

Liam's hand goes to my chin, pulling my gaze to his. "Nothing in that letter says he's dead."

"I know." Pain rips through my pelvic area and I hunch forward, pressing my hand between my thighs. "Oh . . . Oh, Liam."

"What is it, baby? What is it?"

"Call Dr. Murphy. Call her now." I grab the seat back as in front of me another cramp rips through my abdomen and I lose focus for a moment.

"Get her on the line now," Liam is saying urgently into the phone. "I don't care where she is. Just get her."

A damp, sticky sensation forms between my legs, and I look down to see blood seeping through my jeans. "No. No. This can't be happening. Liam, no." I turn to him. "I'm bleeding. I'm bleeding."

Liam curses. "Tellar, get us to the hospital *now*."

Jared curses. "What the fuck is going on back there?"

As Tellar says something to him, Liam pulls me to him and I grab his shirt. "I got you, baby. I got you."

"This is why I didn't want to be pregnant. I lose everyone." My eyes burn, but not nearly as much as my soul. "Everyone. I'll lose you, too, if you stay with me."

"You aren't going to lose me," he promises.

"But you can't tell me I'm not losing the baby, can you?"

He caresses my hair. "Whatever happens, we'll handle it together, baby."

"Wrong answer. Wrong answer." I bury my face in his chest. He was supposed to tell me it's going to be okay, like he always does. Instead, he cups my head and holds me like he's afraid he's going to lose me.

I squeeze my eyes shut, and the dampness clinging to my cheeks and the prickling in my head is a welcome distraction from the cramping in my belly. For once, the past is easier to deal with than the present.

The sound of fire trucks fills the air, and I hurt. Oh God, I hurt all over. It's all there is, but for the smoke. I can't escape the smell, and slowly I become aware of the crackling of flames. Then everything comes back to me. My mother's screams. Mom! I try to lift my head, but I can't. Tears spill from my eyes, and I feel someone's hand on my wrist, then my back.

"Holy fucking shit, tell me she's okay. I need her to be okay."

Chad! I shout in my head at the sound of my brother's voice, but my lungs and throat burn too much for words, and my neck is so very heavy.

"Are you insane, boy?" a man with a familiar voice I can't place demands. "I told you, I'll take care of Lara. Get out of here before they come for you."

"Is my fucking sister okay? I need to know she's okay."

"She's unconscious, but her vitals are good."

"Then I'm taking her with me."

"Is she okay, Dad?" another male voice asks.

"Get the hell out of here, Luke!" the first man shouts. "Go now!"

"But Dad—"

"Go! You saw nothing and no one."

There are footsteps, and the sirens are nearer now. I tell myself to lift my head . . . but I can't.

"You go, too, Chad," the man commands. "Now."

"I'm not leaving without her," Chad repeats.

"She needs a doctor," the man says. "Once I know she's

okay, I'll get her out of the hospital. You just get the paperwork we need."

I awaken with a cramp and hear Liam's urgent voice asking, "Is the baby okay, Doctor?"

I'm in a hospital bed, and a man with gray hair wearing blue scrubs is leaning over me. "I need to run some tests. If you could step out—"

"No." I grab Liam's hand. "I need him here."

"I'm not going anywhere, baby." He levels the doctor with a stare. "I'm staying."

The doctor looks like he wants to argue, but focuses on me. "How do you feel?"

"I'm still cramping, and I think I'm still bleeding."

He studies me intently. "Were you dizzy when you passed out?"

"I have . . . another condition. I black out sometimes."

"Her doctor in New York is treating her for it," Liam says.

"Can we get her doctor on the phone?"

"I did better," Liam says. "She's on a plane headed here."

The doctor looks startled, and I ask, "Dr. Murphy is coming here?"

"Yes. Anything to take care of you, Amy." He glances at the doctor. "She'll be several hours, but I've arranged to have her call from the plane the instant she's airborne."

"Very well," the doctor says and he touches my arm. "In the meantime, we need to get you into a gown and run some tests."

"Does the bleeding mean I'm losing the baby?"

"Not always," he assures me. "We'll know more after the tests. When is your due date?"

"June."

"That puts you close to the three-month mark. We'll be able to check the heartbeat and do a pelvic exam. Have you had a sonogram?"

I shake my head. "Not yet."

"We'll do one today. It's painless, and we'll be able to tell a lot." He glances at Liam. "I'll be at the desk just outside when she's ready."

He steps out and pulls the curtain closed, and Liam kisses my forehead. "Maybe it's just cramps," I say hopefully.

"We'll know soon," he assures me, tugging my shirt over my head and then sliding the gown over my upper body. I still have on the oversized bra from Meg, but I don't care.

Next we remove my pants, and when I see how much blood there is, as hard as I try to fight it, tears slip from my eyes. It's too much blood to just be cramps. I know it is.

Looking grim, Liam grabs the intercom button, punching it and asking for help. Then he wipes my tears. "Hang in there, baby. We're going to get through this."

I cling to his hand for dear life, and looking into his eyes, I see his torment is mine, and while I wish him no pain ever, there is comfort in knowing he isn't just present, but is as deeply wounded by what is happening as I am.

The nurse appears almost instantly and she places something underneath me, then buzzes the doctor.

I grab Liam's hand again and say, "You're still not telling me it's going to be okay."

He caresses a lone tear from my cheek. "I'm supposed to be here for you even when it isn't. I'm going to get the doctor."

I endure the pelvic exam, feeling a bit hopeful when the cramps seem to have eased.

"Well?" Liam asks before I can.

"Your cervix is dilated. That can be an indication of a miscarriage, but let's do the other tests first."

I don't have time to react to the news. A whirlwind of activity follows, through all of which I'm hurting, from heart monitoring to the sonogram, and the doctor and the nurse are incredibly hard to read.

Finally, the doctor says, "I'm very sorry to say that with the level of bleeding, I'm certain that you are miscarrying, and I also recommend a dilation and curettage to ensure you don't hemorrhage excessively. We can wait until your doctor gets here, but if I can talk to her, I'm fairly certain she'll agree."

The rest fades in and out. Something about miscarriages being nothing I did wrong. They can't be explained. I can try again.

By the time the doctor's gone, I'm curled up on my side. Liam climbs on the bed and wraps himself around me. I explode into tears then, my body quaking with the intensity.

TWENTY-FOUR HOURS LATER, it's time to leave the hospital. I shower and dress in the black velour sweatsuit Liam has brought to me along with many of my new things he'd bought me in New York. Trying to feel human, I brush my hair until it's silky and force myself to apply a little makeup.

I emerge from the bathroom to find Liam dressed in a black pinstriped suit with a crisp white shirt and white tie. His dark, thick hair is neatly groomed, his goatee trimmed to perfection, and he's breathtakingly handsome. So very male, when I am feeling like half a woman—but just having him here soothes the ache inside me.

"All right, Mrs. Stone, I just need you to sign some papers. How will you be paying?"

I startle, not having noticed the woman holding a clipboard, she brushes her brown hair from her eyes, presses her black-rimmed glasses up her nose, and nods. "Hello, Mrs. Stone."

Liam's eyes warm, taking on that possessive quality I know so well, and part of me wonders if I'll ever see it again. Without looking away from me, he hands the woman a black American Express. "On my card."

She clears her throat. "Would you like to see the total?"

"No," Liam replies. "I do not want to see the total."

"It's quite large."

He flicks her a look. "I'm good for it."

"Of course. I'll be right back, Mr. Stone."

I glance down at the hospital bracelet on my arm and read the name "Stone." How had I not noticed this before?

Liam steps to me, framing my face with his hands. "I wanted everyone in this town to know I've claimed you. You are mine, and I protect what is mine."

"But I don't. I lost our baby."

"Don't do that to yourself. You didn't do anything. It just wasn't meant to be. We can try again."

"Do you want to try again?"

"If you do."

"I don't know. What if I don't want to, and you do?"

"I just want you, and us, baby. And when the time is

right, I'll ask you to marry me properly and then take you pyramid-hunting all over the world. You and me, baby. That's what I want."

I press to my toes and kiss him. "Thank you."

He wraps his arms around me and I welcome his strength and tenderness. I need him as I have never needed anyone in my life.

"I should be the one thanking you," he murmurs, a rough quality to his voice.

"What are you thanking me for?"

"For being you, and it doesn't matter what name anyone calls you. I love you." His lips quirk. "But I like how Amy Stone sounds. I like it a lot."

I surprise myself and smile, sliding my fingers into that wonderful dark hair of his. "I like it, too."

A knock sounds on the door, and Liam kisses me before calling for the hospital worker to reenter.

"All right," she says. "Here's your receipt; you're all set to go."

Liam turns to take the paperwork, and suddenly the world outside crashes down on me. I'm fantasizing about playing house with Liam, when nothing is solved. We don't know who the stranger I'd seen with my mother is. We don't know if Chad is alive or dead. We haven't dealt with Sheridan Scott.

When the woman pulls the door shut behind her, I lean on the bed. "Now we face my Godzilla again. And I'm pretty sure your sharks are in for the action, too."

Liam steps in front of me. "There's a treatment center in Germany for post-traumatic stress disorder. I thought we'd fly there and make it a vacation."

"No. I'm not running."

"It's not running. It's about you getting well."

"There are doctors in New York."

He studies me a long moment, his expression masked. "You want to go to New York?"

"It's the closest thing I have to a home."

His hand slips under my hair to my neck. "Baby, my home is your home. What's mine is yours."

"I don't want what's yours. I want you, and I want a home. I want stability. I want to walk outside and not fear what's around every corner. So I'm going to do what Chad said. I'm going to talk to Sheridan Scott, and I'm ending this."

"I'm dealing with Sheridan."

"No, Liam. Taking over my life isn't what I need. Just like you told me: together. Remember?"

"I'm trying to take care of you. Chad had the right idea, but my involvement will ensure you're protected."

"Like you said: no excuses. No explanations. Together."

Torment flashes in his eyes. "I'm trying to be the best man I can be for you, Amy. But I don't want you near that man."

I touch his face. "A few minutes ago, I was lost. Then I walked into the room and you were here, and I was found. You do that for me."

"You are my other half, Amy. I have to protect you."

"Just like I want to protect you. But Sheridan Scott knows who I am now. He even knows he can find me with you. This meeting is about closure—and even more, it's my brother's wish, maybe his last one. I need to go."

"What about your health?"

"You made me stay in the hospital a full day, when most people stay a few hours, and I've had Dr. Murphy by my side constantly. I'm allowed to do normal things, within reason. I *really* need to do this, Liam."

He finally nods. "Then we'll go see Sheridan together."

TWENTY

ONCE THAT'S DECIDED, LIAM INSISTS I need to wear something other than the jeans and sweatsuits he brought for me. Dr. Murphy graciously loans me an outfit and, after changing, I exit the bathroom to find her leaning against my hospital bed.

"Liam went to chat with Tellar in the hallway," she says. "How are the shoes?"

"A tad big, but I can make them work."

She gives the fitted, knee-length black dress a once-over, and smiles. "It fits you perfectly."

"Yes. And the color is . . . appropriate."

She presses her red-painted lips together at my obvious reference to mourning. "You *do* know you did nothing wrong, right?"

No, I don't. "If I'd controlled my stress—"

She shakes her head. "There's no scientific data to support a connection between miscarriages and stress. Many women live in horrific circumstances and still deliver at full term."

"The flashbacks—"

"Didn't cause this." She walks over to me, taking my hands in hers. "Sweetie. You did nothing wrong. It just wasn't meant to be."

I hesitate, then say, "When I have flashbacks, they're memories I've forgotten. I don't understand why I don't remember them until I have one of these episodes."

"The mind is an amazing machine. It protects us. It gives us what we can handle. When we get back to New York and you've had some rest, come to my office and we'll talk more."

"Yes. Okay." The idea of visiting her and walking around New York without fear is a good one. I hope this meeting makes that happen.

"Ready?" Liam asks from the doorway.

"Yes," I say, zipping up the bag he's brought me.

Dr. Murphy walks toward Liam. "Make this trip you've

planned fast. I prefer her off her feet." She leaves without waiting for an answer.

Liam arches a brow at me. "I think I've been scolded."

I smile. "Don't mess with Dr. Murphy, or you might *really* get spanked."

He laughs, sauntering toward me, and the wonderful deep, rumbling sound reaches inside me and eases a little of the ache. Wrapping me in his arms, he asks, "You need anything?"

"That's a loaded question."

"I suppose it is. Let's get this meeting over with, and go home."

"Home," I repeat. "I like how that sounds."

"Me too, baby. Me too."

I EXIT THE hospital with an entourage of Liam, Tellar, and Jared. Dr. Murphy is being driven in a private car to the airport to meet us later.

"Sheridan's offices are in Austin," Liam informs me. "Any stops you want to make before we leave?"

"If you mean do I still want to go to the cemetery, the answer is no. When I go, it won't be to say good-bye to all three of them. It will be to tell them I saved my brother."

Understanding fills Liam's eyes. "We'll come back when you're ready."

I lace my fingers with his. "I know." And it feels good to know that he'll be with me.

We ride in silence the rest of the trip. After we've parked in the garage for Sheridan's office building, Liam turns to me and says, "Say nothing inside the garage or the building that you don't want heard. Assume everything is being recorded. You've been through hell, baby, I know, but you can't blink in this meeting. Hold your chin up and be strong. Just your being here sends a message of confidence to Sheridan, but let me talk. Let me handle this."

"Yes."

"Promise me."

"I promise."

"Good." He kisses my forehead and opens the car door.

Tellar and Jared are flanking us almost instantly, and despite having three big, confident men with me, my nerves are fluttering. Some part of me holds on to the hope that this meeting will lead me to my brother. It's all I can think about until I see the well-manned security desk we have to get past in the lobby.

"Give me a minute," Liam says, motioning to Tellar, who falls into step with him, leaving me with Jared.

Jared's eyes land hard on me. "You didn't have to do this."

"Chad's letter didn't tell me to have someone else do this. He said me."

"Because he wasn't sure you'd have anyone else."

"If he left the clue with you, he clearly thought I'd have you."

"And you do. You have me if you need me."

"I know—and I have you to thank for getting me Chad's message, and a whole lot more. I won't ever forget any of it."

"I don't want thanks," he says. "I want you to stay alive."

"Hopefully that's what's about to be guaranteed."

"I know you want your brother back, but that's not going to happen today. Don't get your hopes up. You don't need to be torn down again."

Anger stirs inside me as Liam motions us forward. "Hope is all I have, Jared. Don't take that away from me." I'm borderline furious, and I know it's not about Jared. It's about the fear inside me that I can't contain. "And your timing for this conversation really sucked," I add before I start walking.

"Amy," he calls after me, but I keep going, and when Liam casts me a curious look I don't look at him for fear he'll see me as the stupid wilting flower I feel like right now, before I shake it off. And I will. Before we get to the meeting, I will be a rock.

We step into the elevator and Liam wraps his arm

Lisa Renee Jones

around my waist, a silent show of unity, and it's exactly what I need. I draw a few breaths and find my zone.

The doors open on the twenty-fifth floor and the four of us enter a smaller lobby with a huge oriental rug that softens our footfalls. The lobby is expensively furnished, and like so many downtown Austin offices, the walls are decorated with artwork highlighting the city and state.

A pretty brunette receptionist, with long silky hair touching the shoulders of the pale pink jacket she's paired with a black skirt, stands up to greet us from behind a mahogany desk.

"Mr. Stone," she says tightly, her attention focused on Liam and not because he's every woman's fantasy. There's hostility in her look that I assume should prepare us for more to come.

"I'll show you to Mr. Scott's office."

She flicks a look at Jared and Tellar. "They are not invited."

"That's all right," Jared says, sitting down in a cushy leather chair, draping his arm over the back and settling the ankle of one long, jean-clad leg on his opposite knee. "We'll just keep you company here, sweetheart."

"Sure will," Tellar agrees, claiming a seat across from Jared, stretching his legs out in front of him.

The woman's lips tighten, and it's clear she's not enticed

296

by how good-looking both men are, nor pleased, for that matter. But I am quite pleased. I like knowing they're aware of what's going on.

"This way," the woman says, turning on her heel and walking down a long hallway.

The instant we follow, my nerves are jumping all over the place. Liam's hand settles on my back in a silent assurance of protection and comfort that brings me back down a notch. We're doing this together.

The hallway stops at a walnut-finished double doorway. "This way," the woman says, opening both doors and stepping aside to let us enter.

Liam looks down at me, the promise that we are in this together is in his eyes. Together we walk toward the desk, the centerpiece of a sprawling corner office with a downtown view and expensive walnut furnishings.

Mr. Scott, who's sixty-plus years, with gray hair and a regal carriage, stands as we approach. His lips twist rather wickedly as he says, "Nothing like bringing the mouse to the cat."

"Unless the mouse has become the cat," Liam replies, releasing my hand as he walks forward and sets the large envelope on the desk. "Look inside."

I step to my left to have a view of the two men who have the room crackling with tension. Scott's dark brown eyes narrow on Liam, and he appears just curious enough to bite. He tears open the seal and removes the papers, studying them for a moment. Then he holds up the list of names cut in half. "Where's the other half?"

"It's insurance."

"Insurance?" He crosses his arms. "Go on."

"The complete list, and the damning paperwork attached to it, will be mailed to the Travis County district attorney, the FBI, the CIA, and local law enforcement in the event anything happens to me, Amy, or anyone who has ever breathed the same air as either of us." Liam leans forward and plants his fists on Scott's desk. "But because I'm a paranoid kind of guy, I took it a step further. I put a price on your head, and on every name on that list."

I gape. A price? As in he hired a hit man? Surely not.

Scott leans in and plants his hands on the desk just as Liam has. "Two can play that game. A price for a price."

"Then we go nuclear," Liam replies.

"Yes," Scott agrees. "We go nuclear."

Liam pushes off the desk and returns to my side, his hand on my waist. "Let's go."

He starts to turn me, but Scott looks at me for the first time since I've entered the room, and the cold calculation in his eyes sets me off. "I want my brother back," I demand.

"It takes a miracle to raise the dead, little one," he replies. "And I don't see you offering me any motivation to create one."

"I have nothing to offer," I reply. "I was never part of this. I never knew anything. I still don't."

His jaw sets, and he reaches for a picture and turns it to face us. My lips part in shock as I stare at the stranger we've been trying to find.

"My son. He was killed tragically in a plane crash six years ago. Your brother was with him. So I guess we can all agree: your brother's future has always been in his own hands. But if I could have helped him, I would have. Just as I'm sure you would have."

"She has nothing you want," Liam bites out. "But if I find out you have what she wants, you'll regret the day you were born. And I will find out."

"Because you have money?" He laughs. "So do I."

"Money has nothing to do with it. It's what I'm willing to do, and capable of doing, to protect what's mine. Push me and I will make you bleed in ways you never believed possible." Liam turns me to the door and we start walking.

"Mr. Stone."

Liam pauses with his hand on the door handle.

"It's you who doesn't know what I'm capable of."

Liam's lips hint at a cynical smile, and he turns to face

Scott. "Not everything. But there are at least a hundred ways I *do* know you in that paperwork, and all of those ways are illegal. Read through the documents, and butter up some popcorn. There are some real blockbusters in there."

And this time, we leave.

Tellar and Jared follow us into the elevator car, and the need for silence is killing me. The instant we're in the SUV I turn to Liam, but then decide not to speak, afraid I might say something that could later incriminate him.

He leans in, resting his cheek next to mine, and whispers, "Yes. I really did it. I will do anything to protect you and make you happy. Anything."

SHORTLY AFTER WE arrive at the private section of the airport, Dr. Murphy arrives, and Tellar helps her with her bags.

Jared turns to Liam and me. "This is where I say goodbye."

"What about Chad?" I ask. "We need your help."

"I'll look for Chad my own way."

"Why not join us?" Liam asks. "Consider it a private-hire job."

"I freelance for a reason. I work best by myself." He

flicks a look at Liam. "The jury is still out on you for me, Stone." Then his gaze settles on me. "Take care, Amy." He turns and heads toward the building.

I go after him. "Wait! Wait!"

Looking surprised, he faces me, and I say, "You're the way Chad reaches me."

"If Chad calls, I'll be in touch." He softens his voice. "You can't live thinking Chad will reappear, Amy. That's not living—and that's not what Chad wanted for you."

Wanted. Past tense. He thinks Chad's dead. "And you can't live without hope, Jared—or you won't be living at all."

His lips quirk, the wind blowing wisps of hair from the clasp at the back of his neck. "I haven't really lived in a long time. I'll be in touch."

This time I let him go.

When Liam steps to my side and laces his fingers through mine, I tell him, "He left because he thinks Chad's dead."

"He left because this isn't his place, or his way. Not because of Chad. And it doesn't mean either of them is gone." He motions to the plane. "We need to get you off your feet."

I nod and let him lead me onto the private plane we've been on once before. Dr. Murphy fusses over me for a while, and finally Liam and I settle into seats in the back of the cabin, the curtain pulled shut for privacy. With a blanket and a pillow, I lie on my side facing Liam, and he faces me. The engines roar to life, and I think about how much has happened since that first time I saw Liam in the New York airport, and sat next to him on that plane.

I ask, "That flight to Denver—did you have anything to do with my ending up in first class?"

"Of course I did. I asked if you were making it onto the flight, and was told yes, there was one coach seat left. I paid the guy sitting next to me in first class fifty thousand dollars to take it."

I gape. "You paid fifty thousand dollars to sit next to me? You were flying commercial. You could have flown private for that."

"I fly commercial often—I don't believe in throwing my money away. But that fifty thousand dollars was the best money I've ever spent."

"But you didn't know me."

He reaches over and strokes my cheek. "When our eyes met in that airport, I saw another lost soul. And baby, you'll never be alone again."

I curl my fingers on his cheek and smile. "*We'll* never be alone again."

TWENTY-ONE

LIAM AND I SPEND THE ENTIRE flight home talking about pyramids, and I find myself excited to talk about my family and the many amazing things I experienced with them. To honor them, as Liam had once suggested.

By the time we walk into our home I'm exhausted, but I'm eager to gobble down a pizza in bed with him. And when he calls it "our habit," it creates a sweet, warm spot in my chest. Not since I lived at home with my family have I had habits I shared with anyone.

I fall asleep in Liam's arms, feeling safer than I have in a long time. But as I drift off to sleep I can't help but think of Chad and wonder where he is.

"Honey, grab the mail?" my mom asks as she stirs a pan on the stove. "I'm expecting something important."

"Sure, Mom," I say, pushing away from the table where I was doing my homework.

Humming the new song I'd just downloaded off of iTunes, I head toward the porch. I'll never get used to my mom baking cakes rather than digging in the dirt beside my dad.

"You're fucking my mother? Are you insane?"

I stop at the sound of my brother's angry outburst, shocked.

"You fucked me," another male replies. "I wanted to show you how easily I can fuck you, and anyone near you. She thinks she's helping to convince me to let your father out of our deal." He gives a low laugh.

A rough growl escapes Chad's lips and he shoves the man against the wall. "You touch my mother, or anyone in my family again, and I'll kill you."

"You give me what's mine—or you and your family will all be dead."

"I don't have it."

"You'd better get it, then."

"I told you, I didn't take it."

"What's going on?"

I jump at the sound of my mother's voice behind me. She steps to the screen door and I hear a soft gasp escape her lips. She shoves open the door and repeats, "What's going on?"

The stranger Chad was fighting with is walking down the stairs, and I can't see his face.

"You tell me, Mom," Chad says, confronting her. "Get a little too lonely while we were away?"

I hug myself, fighting tears. This isn't happening. But I saw her with the man in the black sedan. I saw her, and—

"I tried to clean up your and your father's mess," my mother says, her voice shaking.

"You got used like a cheap washcloth."

My mother gasps at Chad's harsh words and bursts into tears, rushing through the door and past me.

Chad tries to follow her but I step in front of him, swiping at tears, anger surging through my body. "What did you do? What did you both do?"

"I told you, you can't handle it."

"What did you do, Chad?"

He looks at the ceiling, torment and self-hatred pouring off of him. Then he grabs my arms, stares at me a moment, and kisses my forehead. "I'll fix this. I promise you, Lara. I'll fix it. Everything is going to be okay."

I wake up, instantly aware of Liam holding me tight

against his body, one leg wrapped around mine, and I realize why I hate the promise that everything's going to be okay. I hate it because of that day.

And yet I *am* okay. I have Liam, and I have survived.

It's my brother whose survival is in question.

EPILOGUE

DRIP. DRIP. DRIP.

"Fuck! Fuck. Fuck. Fuck."

I lift my aching head, which feels like a hundred pounds on my stiff neck, and stare at the concrete walls of what has become my cage. Where is that fucking noise coming from?

Drip. Drip.

Losing my mind, I tug at my hands behind my back, the rope biting into my flesh. "Fuckkkkkk!"

My head drops between my shoulders and I stare at the ground.

Drip. Drip.

Red dots clutter my gaze, and I focus on the red puddle beneath me. Blood. Oh, yeah. I'm bleeding.

The door opens with a loud grinding of metal and I squeeze my eyes shut, ready to die, hoping it's time. If Jared did what he was supposed to do and saved Lara, it will be. She deserves to live. I don't. But I won't go out a coward.

Defiantly, I lift my head, and I think I blink. My eyelids are too swollen to be sure. Considering there's a gorgeous brunette in a black dress that hugs her curves in all the right places standing in front of me, maybe I'm already dead. Her creamy ivory skin and pale blue eyes are pretty angelic, so yeah, I think I'm dead. Fuck, though—I still hurt all over, so I must've gotten what I deserve. I'm in hell, and the devil is a hot bitch playing games with me. I could think of worse nightmares. Like my life.

Drip. Drip.

But the dead don't bleed, and I sure the fuck am. I give the bitch a smirk, eyeing her with a long inspection meant to make her feel uncomfortable and send me to my hell with at least a little pleasure.

"Sweetheart, you're going to need a whole lot more than stilettos and great legs to get me to talk—though I'm pretty sure I have some moans left in me. I'll let you have a few, too."

She pulls a knife out from behind her back.

"Ah," I murmur. "You like it kinky, do ya? I guess this is where things get interesting."

"Yes, Chad," she replies, her voice as sexy as her legs. "It is."

And then she, and her knife, move just where I want them: nice and close.

Amy's brother, Chad, has done everything in his power to protect his sister and save what he has left of his family. Knowing that escaping his captor will only put his family back in danger, he has to try and end this thing once and for all. There's just one problem—the woman who helped him escape either loves him or wants him dead.

Don't miss the next installment in
The Secret Life of Amy Bensen series
from *New York Times* bestselling author Lisa Renee Jones

Forsaken

Coming summer 2015 from Gallery Books!

DRIP. DRIP. DRIP.

I lift my aching head and stare at the concrete walls of my prison. Where is that goddamn unending sound coming from?

Drip. Drip.

Feeling like I'm losing my mind, I tug at my hands behind my back, the rope biting into my flesh. "Fuuuck!"

My head drops between my shoulders and I stare at the ground.

Drip. Drip.

Red dots clutter my gaze and I focus on the puddle beneath me. Blood. I'm bleeding. That's why the hair hanging in my eyes is red instead of blond.

The door opens with a loud grinding of metal and I squeeze my eyes shut, ready to die, hoping Jared did what he was supposed to do and saved Lara. She deserves to live. I don't. But I will not go out a coward.

Defiantly, I lift my head and blink my swollen eyelids and see . . . a gorgeous brunette in a slim-cut black skirt that hugs her curves in all the right places? Maybe I'm dead already. Her creamy ivory skin and pale blue eyes are pretty angelic—so yeah, I must be dead. I still hurt all over, though, so I must have gotten what I deserve. I'm in hell, and the devil is a hot bitch playing games with me.

Drip. Drip.

Or not. The dead don't bleed—which means she's one of Sheridan's minions. I give her a smirk, eyeing her with a lengthy inspection meant to make her feel uncomfortable and to send me to my hell with at least a little pleasure.

"Sweetheart, you're going to need a whole lot more than stiletto heels and great legs to get me to talk. But I'm pretty sure I have some moans left in me. I'll let you have a few, too."

She pulls a knife out from behind her back. "Ah," I say, "you like it kinky? I guess this is where things get interesting."

"Yes, Chad," she murmurs, her voice as sexy as her body. "It is." And then she and her knife move to just where I want them. Nice and close, the steel pressed to my jawline, my five-day stubble proving to be a layer of protection I doubt she's counting on. Her eyes meet mine and they are cold, blue, and unreadable. The kind of eyes that make a man want to fuck a woman until she begs for more, just to prove he can do it. I wait for the blade to cut me. I hope for it, but it doesn't come.

"Get naked, sweetheart," I order roughly, intent on getting under her skin and ensuring that I win this hand of poker, not her. "At least then you'll have my attention. It'll give whoever's watching through that camera in the corner the thrill of a lifetime, too."

Apparently not intimidated, she settles her hands on my shoulders, still holding the blade. I'm just about to make a smart-ass comment about her breasts when she brings her knee between my legs, giving my groin a calculated nudge. "Now do I have your attention?" she hisses.

"Good try," I reply glibly, pretending I didn't just have an *oh shit* moment, "but I prefer your hand, or other body parts. I'm certain you would, as well."

A frustrated sound purrs in her throat, sexy enough to get

me hard if she hadn't just caused my balls to retract damn near to my nipples. "This isn't a game," she bites out, thankfully dropping her knee rather than planting it, but her fingers and the handle of the knife remain on my shoulders. "Sheridan might need you alive to get what he wants," she continues, "but you underestimate him if you think he won't start chopping off body parts."

At the mention of my bastard captor, all fun and games are over. My jaw clamps down, shoulders bunching beneath her touch. "Your boss knows the rules of my organization. If I show up anywhere near the people who can get him what he wants and I'm less than a hundred percent, I'll be considered compromised. It'll be snatched out of my reach faster than I could make you scream my name, and that's fast, baby."

"There are ways to hurt you that won't be seen. You know it. He knows it. He'll make you talk." She leans forward, pressing her cheek to mine, and a sweet floral scent teases my nostrils while her long brown hair slips over my face as she whispers, "I can't let you tell him where it is."

She shoves off me, standing with the blade at her side, my blood staining her pale cheek, tension blasting off her. She looks determined, pissed off even, and for survival's sake I have to assume she means to act on her proclamation to ensure that I don't talk. Which leaves me with only one question. What will she do to ensure I keep my mouth shut? The thought has me suddenly giving new respect to the knife in her hand.

"He can't make me talk," I promise her. "He's tried."

"You're good," she counters, using my words against me. "But I promise you, you're not *that* good." She doesn't wait for a response, walking around me, disappearing out of sight a moment before one of her hands comes back down on my shoulder. I steel myself for the blade, calm, even at peace. This is the right way to go, dying to protect a secret I should never have unearthed in the first place. A secret that could destroy or save the world. I don't want to be the one who makes that decision.

Then an image of my sister's face fills the empty space of my mind, and the innocence in her eyes shreds me. I don't know if Jared got to Lara in time to protect her, and even if he did, Sheridan now knows she's alive. He'll think she has the secret that only I hold, and he'll go after her. Others will, too. I'm the only one she has to protect her—though she doesn't know I'm still alive.

My fight returning, I try to look over my shoulder. "Don't be a coward. Face me if you mean to use that knife." The instant I make the demand, a loud blast shakes the ceiling and smoke starts forming by my feet, fast consuming the room.

The woman shakes me by my shoulders, shouting, "What did you do? What did you do?"

Since my hands are tied, we both know she's responsible for the smoke grenade that just went off, but I give her an A for acting skills.

She moves in front of me, jerking my head to one side. "What did you *do*?"

My eyes narrow on hers. "Payback's a bitch," I promise.

As the smoke consumes us her hands come down on my knees, and it's clear she's squatting in front of me. "What the—?" I begin as she cuts free one of my legs and then the other.

Then she leans into me, pushing herself to her feet, her hand on to my shoulder as if she's afraid of losing me in the smoke. Freedom is so close I can taste it, adrenaline is pouring through me like liquid fire. She grabs my forearm, and every muscle in my body is tense as I wait for my bindings to be cut. Instead, there's a plastic cuff attached to my wrist that I instinctively know is about to be connected to her arm as well.

"Don't even think about it," I growl, using all of my energy to jerk the chair that barely moves. The original binding between my arms goes slack and I'm on my feet in an instant, feeling the weight of her arm connected to mine. Cursing, I yank her hard against me and reach for the knife, only to hear the clanging of steel on the concrete floor somewhere in the smoke cloud.

"Bitch." I cup the back of her head, pulling her ear to my lips. "You just made a mistake you're going to regret."

Her fingers curl around my shirt. "I couldn't let you leave me here," she hisses fiercely. "He'll kill me."

"Don't be so sure I won't," I counter, dragging her to the door and pulling it open. Sheridan doesn't want me dead. My guess is he wants me to escape with this woman, whom he wants to seduce me into taking him to his treasure.

I stop inside the door frame, inching around it to see that we're inside an unfinished office space in a windowless basement level. "This way," the woman says, moving in front of me and taking a step.

With my feet firmly planted, she is promptly jerked back to me, at which point I demand, "What happened to pretending I was forcing you to help me?"

She swipes her long brown hair from her eyes. "There's no camera past the doorway and whatever you think I'm up to, I'm not. I'm just trying to stay alive."

"And keep me from talking," I add flatly. My belief in her story is right up there with Santa Claus. "How many men up top?"

"Ten in the warehouse and another ten in the lab, but the explosion should have blocked the door between them and us. I can't be sure. I winged it."

I arch a brow. "You did this on your own?"

"Yes. I didn't have time to come up with anything else when I heard what they were planning. We should be able to take the emergency stairs and exit into the back alley, but we have to hurry."

"What city are we in?"

Ignoring my questions, she insists, "We have to go!"

"What city are we in?" I demand again, no give in my voice.

"Austin. This is where—"

"Sheridan runs his oil empire. I know." A long way from Denver, where I was captured. "What part of Austin?"

"Downtown," she replies as we cross the unfinished concrete floor. "When we exit into the hallway, we'll take the stairs and then go left. The door that should be blocked is to the right; it leads to the main warehouse."

"What's outside the exit?"

"An alleyway off Seventh Street. That exit is the only way in or out now, and trouble could be waiting for us there. They'll call for reinforcements."

"I'm good at handling trouble—something you'd do well to remember, since you fit that description." We stop at the exit door and I turn to look her in the eyes. "I can think of twenty different ways the next five minutes can go, and in nineteen of them, you die. In eighteen, I'm the one who kills you."

"Then you'll have to drag my body along with you."

"Good exercise, sweetheart. As Clint says: 'Make my day.'"

While her glare says anger, there's a flicker of fear deep in those blue eyes. The kind of fear I have nightmares about seeing in Lara's eyes. Maybe Sheridan isn't so stupid, since a woman's betrayal got me here in the first place. And this one is smart.

Frustrated, I inch forward to study the hallway. Sure enough, smoke pours from a steel door to the right. But it's contained, which tells me Sheridan's men hit it with an extinguisher before it could draw attention, or . . . this is all a setup.

Irritated all over again, I quickly go through the door, and we're up the stairs and then outside in the empty alleyway in a matter of seconds.

"My car is parked on the street down there," the woman says, pointing to the right. I go left. "My car," she insists, stumbling in her high heels as she tries to keep up.

"Will be tracked."

"No. I told you, I'm not with Sheridan."

"Do you work for him?"

"Yes."

I don't look at her. "And you know about what he's looking for?"

"Yes, but—"

"Then your car's being tracked." We round a corner and I scan the street; it's nighttime, all the businesses closed, the streets deserted.

"We'll be spotted here." She lifts our wrists. "Look at us."

"Take off your shoes," I order.

"What? I need—"

"I don't have time to argue." My fingers span her tiny waist as I lift her, peel off her high heels with my foot, and then bend down to scoop them up. "We need to get to the other side of the highway quickly," I say, handing them to her.

"That's East Austin. It's dangerous and—"

I start moving, giving her no choice but to keep up while I battle limited vision in my left eye from the swelling. I can handle a rough neighborhood to escape Sheridan.

We reach the highway and I make sure we dart across traffic against the light, putting distance and the major thoroughfare between us and Sheridan's warehouse, and quickly trek up a hill toward the neighborhood beyond it.

"This is gang turf," the woman warns. "It's dangerous. And can you even see? Your eye—"

"*I'm* fucking dangerous," I growl, "and your boss is equivalent to the kingpin of these so-called gangs."

"He's not my boss, and I'm serious about this neighborhood. We can't walk around here even in daylight."

"It's not safe, but it's the right place to get lost with a woman cuffed to your arm and not have the cops called on you." I cut her a hard look. "So I suggest you keep quiet so we won't draw attention we don't want." We top the hill and I spot the piñata shop that's the marker for gang town. Everything beyond it is colored territories, a bitch fight waiting to happen. As we approach, a fortysomething Mexican man is closing the gate to the fenced-in yard.

He pauses, tracking our approach, and when we stop on the other side of the gate his intelligent eyes meet mine, no doubt taking in my beaten face and then shifting to the woman next to me, who still has my blood on her cheek. He glances at the cuffs that join us, gives a snort, and returns his attention to me.

"Qué chingados paso?" he demands. *What the fuck happened?*

In Spanish, I give my quick and outrageous explanation and plea for help. He listens intently, his eyes going wide, sympathy filling them, before he introduces himself and invites us inside, opening the gate.

My ball and chain looks up at me, the streetlight illuminating her expressive eyes. "What did you say to him?"

"Do you really want to know?"

"Yes." Either she doesn't know Spanish or she's a damn good actress.

"Too bad." When she doesn't move, I grab her arm and drag her along with me, murmuring an apology to Hugo, as he claims to be called, and explaining to him that she's embarrassed.

He shuts the gate and walks ahead of us to a broken-down house, then opens the door.

"This is dangerous," the woman murmurs.

"He's not as dangerous as I am," I promise, following Hugo into a room that's been converted into a storefront with a counter and a cash register, and pass through to a very seventies puke-green kitchen. Hugo walks to a drawer and removes a pair of scissors, then hands them to me with instructions to use the spare bedroom and bath down the hallway to clean up.

"Telephone?" he asks in English.

"No," I say quickly.

A knowing look settles in Hugo's eyes and he nods. Thanking him, I accept a first aid kit, and urge the woman toward the door to our right. She opens it and I follow her inside the small bedroom that's simple but clean, with a door to what he's told me is a bathroom. I shut us inside the bedroom and toss the woman's shoes and the first aid kit onto the rainbow-colored Mexican blanket on the twin bed. The woman grabs the plastic between our wrists, as if trying to stop me from cutting us apart.

"Move your hand or I'll cut it," I warn, blood trickling irritatingly down my cheek. "We don't have much time, and we can't leave with these cuffs on."

"You can't leave me."

"Says who? Besides Sheridan."

"Me." Her voice quakes. "I say."

I narrow my eyes at her, or I think I do. I can't feel one of my eyelids and—damn it to hell—blood drips down onto my arm. "What's in this for you?"

"I told you: I don't want him to get what he's after. And how do you know that man who helped us isn't calling the police or some gang right now?"

I ignore her question and my desire to ask her a few of my own. "Move your hand."

"You're bleeding again, badly."

"*Move* your hand."

"Please," she whispers. "Don't leave me behind. I gambled on you helping me when I chose your silence over Sheridan's demands. He doesn't forgive or forget, and I don't know how to re-create my identity and hide. I don't know what to do."

The desperation in her voice just annoys me; it reminds me of that lying bitch, Meg. I'd fallen for her damsel-in-distress routine, and she'd turned out to be Sheridan's puppet. The thought spurs me to anger and action, and I reach under her arm and grab her elbow, twisting our arms and forcing her to let go of the cuff. Wasting no time, I cut the plastic tying us together and then make fast work of the bracelet remaining on her arm, then the three on mine. Unwilling to let her get her hands on the scissors, and not ready to let go of my only weapon, I shove them in my pocket.

My hands come down on the wall on either side of her head and I stare down into her sky blue eyes, fear in their depths that she tries to hide with a defiant lift of her chin. Her bravado is my undoing, a reminder of my sister. Lara is nothing like this woman, who has experience and secrets in her eyes, but it doesn't seem to matter. This stranger and assumed enemy keeps making me think of her anyway. And that's a dangerous path I'm not letting myself travel.

"You're in the forest with wolves, woman, and even if you think you're one of us, you're not. We'll *all* eat you alive. Get out before I have you for dinner."

Shoving away from her, I swipe some blood from my face and grab the first aid kit from the bed. I've only taken a step toward the bathroom when it hits me that she could be wearing a wire or a tracking device.

Turning to face her again, I shackle her wrist and pull her into the tiny bathroom that holds just a toilet and a sink. Placing her in front of the sink and mirror, I step behind her, my hands framing the dip at her waist, and I'm far from oblivious of the curvy but slender hips, and her round, perfect backside. Both assets are reasons Sheridan would pick her for this job, no doubt.

Fuming at the thought, my eyes meet hers in the mirror and I see panic in hers that no one fakes. Good. She should be panicked right now. "What are you going to do?" she demands.

"Dinner came early."

She tries to turn but I step into her, pinning her between my thighs, her soft round backside now against my groin. My cock reacts like it's just been given a reward, thickening instantly, not giving a flying fuck that she's Sheridan's bitch.

"Let me go," she demands.

"You just ordered me to do the opposite in the other room."

"I told you not to leave me behind—not pin me against a bathroom sink."

She tries to shift again, and my zipper stretches to painful limits. "Enough," I grind out. "I need to be sure you aren't wired."

She stills, her eyes meeting mine in the mirror again. "Wired? A tracking device? No. I don't have either."

"Forgive me if I don't take you at your word."

"What you are going to do?" she asks again, the panic in her eyes now audible in the quiver of her voice.

"I'm going to find out for myself—and we can do that one of two ways." I turn her to face me, my legs clamping around hers again instantly, my hands returning to her waist, where I intentionally flex my fingers. "I can search you, intimately and completely." I pause for effect. "Or you can strip down and prove you're clean."

Her lips part in a silent gasp. "You can't be serious."

"As serious as a wolf about to rip out a deer's throat, sweetheart, and this needs to happen now. Which will it be?"

"Sheridan wouldn't have me wear a wire. He'd know you'd do this."

"Of course he does—the whole idea here is for me to get you naked. He wants you in my bed. And if you're offering, I won't decline, but it'll be me fucking you—not you fucking me."

"I'm not offering anything." Her hands press hard against my chest. "Let me out of here."

"Not a problem," I say, doing no doubt the opposite of what she expects—releasing her and moving the few inches away the space allows.

But we're still close, a few inches separating us at best, and I can smell the damnable floral scent of her skin. She grips the sink behind her, her chest rising and falling in steady, heavy movements, but she doesn't leave. Of course not. She works for Sheridan. Even if she wants to go, she can't.

I make a grand gesture toward the door. "Feel free. You're on your own."

Indecision flickers over her face, that streak of my blood a drastic contrast to her beautiful porcelain skin. Damn it to hell, why am I noticing her skin? Irritated at myself and at her, my hands go to her waist and I lift her and set her aside. Stepping to the sink, I grab the towel on the rack and turn on the water.

"What are you doing?" she asks.

I glance up at her. "That question is getting old but if you must know, I'm cleaning up to get the hell out of here. And so we're clear, I'm leaving without you."

"If you think I'm being tracked, why aren't you leaving now?"

"Because you being wired means Sheridan set this escape up and he only wants to keep an eye on us. In which case I actually have more time, not less."

"Then you need to know you have less. I'm not wearing a

tracking device." She grabs my arm. "I'm also not the whore you seem to think I am. I can't get naked to prove it."

The conviction in her voice is pretty damn believable, and so is the desperation in her eyes, but why wouldn't it be? Failing Sheridan comes with a steep price.

"Suit yourself," I say, bending over the sink to splash water on my face. Then I soap up my arms and my face, irritating the gash on my cheek, which starts oozing blood all over again. "Fuck." I turn off the water and reach for the first aid kit, aware that I need stitches.

"Why are you still here?" I demand of the woman, grabbing two Band-Aids out of the kit.

"I don't know where to go."

"And yet you acted damn confident when you were working me over for the camera."

"My hands were shaking, and I was terrified."

"Well, you put on a good show, sweetheart. You made it look like I kidnapped you."

"Yes, in case I was captured—but he's not easily fooled. Please. I need help. I just . . . do what you have to do to believe me. Pat me down. It's better than getting naked. I think. I hope. Just get it over with."

It's all the invitation I need. I pull her back to the sink, in front of me, my legs again shackling hers. She twists her fingers in my shirt, her lashes lowered, dark stains on her pale cheeks.

"Look at me," I order, trying to figure out why I can't turn on the ice in my veins with this woman.

Her eyes open, chin lifting, and I remind myself that I have every reason to make this hard on her . . . except one. The vulnerable, shaken look in her eyes.

I squat down in front of her, wrapping my hands around her slender ankles, where I linger, reminding myself that I need to treat her like a hostile. This needs to make her uncomfortable. But I can't help but think of my sister, whose life was ripped out from under her by no choice or action of her own. The idea that this woman could be a victim like Lara doesn't sit well.

Letting out a heavy breath I begin to explore her body, running my hands up her legs to the top of her thigh-highs, where I search the elastic for a hidden device. Next, I move up her hips, and she sucks in a breath as I run my fingers between her thighs. She's wearing a thong, but as tempting as her ass might be, this isn't about sex or taking advantage of her. If I were certain she was Sheridan's bitch, though, the story would be different.

Trying not to give either of us time to think about the invasion this is for her, if she truly is innocent in all this, I stand up and turn her to face the mirror again. She drops her head forward, her long, silky brown hair draping her face. I tug her black silk blouse from her skirt and my fingers tunnel underneath, deftly searching her slender waist, ribs, and the sides of her breasts. I hesitate a moment . . . and then do what has to be done, searching the most obvious hiding place for a tracking or recording device. Cupping her breasts, I feel nothing but curves and woman. When I shove down the lace cups, ensuring there's nothing inside, she pants. Hell, I think I do too, and I remove my hands to tangle my fingers in her hair, parting it and searching her neckline.

Finally, I turn her to face me all over again, planting my hands on either side of her. She stares down, as far from playing a seductress as you can get, but that doesn't mean she isn't playing me. Still, she's not wearing a device, and I find myself saying, "I had to do that."

Her gaze jerks to mine, her cheeks flushed. "I know," she

whispers, delicately clearing her throat. "I get it. I . . . appreciate that you didn't—"

"Don't. Don't appreciate anything, because I'll turn on you in a minute flat if you give me a flicker of a reason. I don't trust you."

"And I don't trust you."

"You shouldn't. What's your name?"

"Gia Hudson."

"Is that your real name?"

I don't miss the two beats of hesitation or the lowering of her lashes before she says, "Of course it's my real name." Her gaze finds mine. "Is Chad yours?"

I ignore the question. "What were you doing with Sheridan in the first place?"

A knock sounds on the door of the bedroom.

"Clean the blood off your face," I order as I head through the small bedroom, my nerve endings buzzing and my damn cock still hard. Cautiously, I crack the door open to find a teenage boy who resembles Hugo standing in the hallway.

"Trouble, señor," he says. "There are men searching the neighborhood. My father turned down the lights and bolted the door, but he says you should leave out the back."

I curse under my breath. "We're going." I turn to get Gia, but she's already here, her shoes in hand.

"I heard," she says. "And 'we' better mean you and me, because you aren't leaving me. Not after I just let you search me."

The smart thing to do would be to just leave her. The odds of her being part of a setup are overwhelmingly strong, but she wasn't bugged. And if she really has crossed Sheridan, he'll kill her.

"You do exactly what I say, when I say it. Understand?"

She swallows hard. "Yes. I understand. I will."

"Fuck with me, and I'll fuck you over ten times worse." My warning issued, I grab her wrist and enter the hallway.

I can almost see Sheridan's laughing face and hear him calling me a fool, but it doesn't seem to matter. I've made up my mind. This woman is coming with me—until I decide what to do with her.